The Mad Detective

by the same author

GIVE UP THE GHOST
JOSEPHINE
JONAH'S MIRROR
AN ASH-BLONDE WITCH
FULL MOON
SELKIE
ISABEL'S DOUBLE
WHAT BECKONING GHOST
YOUNG MAN OF MORNING

for younger children

THE REAL LIVE DINOSAUR AND OTHER STORIES
GABRIELLE
THE HALLOWE'EN CAT

The Mad Detective

KENNETH
LILLINGTON

faber and faber
LONDON · BOSTON

For Janice

First published in 1992
by Faber and Faber Limited
3 Queen Square London WC1N 3AU

Photoset by Wilmaset Ltd, Wirral
Printed in England by Clays Ltd, St Ives plc

© Kenneth Lillington, 1992

Kenneth Lillington is hereby identified as author of this work
in accordance with Section 77 of the Copyright,
Designs and Patents Act 1988

A CIP record for this book is available from the British Library

ISBN 0 571 16593 1

Mr Glossop hated his own name. It was, of course, a perfectly good one – there were five other Glossops in the telephone directory, all no doubt rejoicing in it – but this was no help to him. He felt that if ever a story were written about him, it would have to be some sort of knock-about farce. He tampered with certain celebrated tragedies: Glossop the Prince of Denmark; Glossop and Juliet; even Anna Glossopenina; but this only made it sound more absurd. And because a name defines its owner, he in a way hated himself.

Perhaps the cause lay in his infancy. In the Infants' School there was a group of squeaky little girls who made a butt of him. They would dance round him in a ring chanting in an idiotic singsong, 'Reggie Glossop is a sausage!' It was no good his pointing out that this statement was without foundation, because that only excited them further, and they would cross their eyes and hang out their tongues with hilarious disrespect, and giggle until they collapsed in hysterical heaps. This humiliated him so much that, as he grew older, he buried it deeper in his subconscious mind than ever a murderer buried a corpse.

His sense of unworthiness drove him to strive feverishly for worldly success. He crammed his early years with toil, and by middle age he had become the proprietor of a great hotel in the rural Cotswolds. It towered over the arty-crafty village, and flushed the western sky with neon sunsets after dark.

He was the king of his world. But still he was not happy. By now, sadly, he had developed a persecution complex of an appalling kind. It took the form of a fear of women.

On this particular morning, Mr Glossop slunk into the backroom office of the Staff Manager, Mrs Hailstone, and crept to the window, through which he peered as fearfully as if expecting a sniper's bullet. Mrs Hailstone, typing on the other side of the room, did not look up from her machine.

He relaxed, made a pad of his handkerchief, and dabbed his brow, but in the very next instant he stiffened and cowered back as a figure in the street below came into view.

'There's another one!'

Mrs Hailstone finished her letter, gave it a little nod of approval, removed it from her typewriter and placed it with its envelope in her out-tray. Only then did she rise and, without hurrying, walk over to the window to look down the sheer back of the hotel on its steep grassy bank.

'Mr Glossop, that is just a common or garden woman, doing her shopping and minding her own business.'

'What business?'

'She is buying some bananas.'

'How do I know she isn't bluffing?'

'Mr Glossop, she doesn't know you exist!'

'I can't be sure, you see,' said Mr Glossop tragically. 'I can never be sure.'

'Mr Glossop,' said Mrs Hailstone, with the very slightest impatience, 'are you sure your fears are justified? Why do women hunt you? What's in it for them? Is the general stock of men exhausted? Or how would you explain it?'

'Yes,' said Mr Glossop, on a new note of philosophical

interest, 'it *is* an interesting question. It may be my adorable clumsiness. I seldom enter a room without stumbling and knocking over something valuable. Women can't resist that in a man.'

'Oh,' said Mrs Hailstone. It was on account of Mr Glossop's clumsiness that all the antiques in the hotel had been replaced with reproductions, and she personally did not find it adorable. 'Well, will you sign this letter? And now, Mr Glossop, I have to interview someone, so would you mind . . . ?'

He nodded submissively and left her room, only to spring back in consternation.

'There's one in the corridor!'

'Ah, that'll be my interviewee,' said Mrs Hailstone. 'She's come about a holiday job.'

'Oh,' said Mr Glossop, relaxing. He did not regard female members of staff as women. But he stiffened again. 'Suppose it's one of Them infiltrating?'

Mrs Hailstone drew a deep breath and counted five. 'Of course, I could engage male staff only,' she said, 'but you never know, it might be one of Them in drag.'

'My God yes,' said Mr Glossop, and began to punctuate his speech with hyphens. 'One – couldn't hide – *anywhere* . . . Female staff – safer – yes. Even so – ' and he put on a pair of dark glasses and turned his coat collar up. This did not disguise him in the least, but it made him look rather sinister. He re-entered the corridor, where stood a young girl who looked rather taken aback. At his second appearance she looked quite startled, but Mrs Hailstone went smilingly to the door and drew her into the room.

'Harriet Gardiner? Do come in.'

'It's all right, my dear,' she added, as Harriet Gardiner cast an uncertain look at the door. 'Our proprietor is rather restless, but there's no need to be afraid of him. *Do* sit down.'

*

'Quite a classical beauty,' thought Mrs Hailstone, taking stock of Harriet Gardiner. Her photograph would not have been out of place in one of those 'country' magazines that adore the upper classes. One visualized: 'The Hon. Harriet Gardiner, recently engaged to marry Rupert, the son of Col and Lady Ffanshaw-Ffanshaw.' Except that there was no pose about her. She had a fresh, sweet, open look. Mrs Hailstone took an instant liking to her.

'So your parents run Gardiners, the antiques shop in the village, Harriet,' she said. 'Are you going to follow in their footsteps?'

'Oh no,' said Harriet decidedly, 'not me.'

'Don't you like antiques – beautiful things?'

'Oh yes, but I don't like to see them priced.'

'Well,' said Mrs Hailstone, liking her even more, 'I don't have to tell you that the village attracts a lot of collectors, and this hotel is full of them, and most of them do judge things by their price. Between you and me, it's sometimes hard to tell the genuine from the phoney. What are you going to do, Harriet?'

'I'm going to university to read biology.'

'Ah! That really does get down to basics.'

She outlined Harriet's duties and set her on course, and, smiling at the pleasant impression the girl had left, she sat down at her desk and riffled through the morning's mail. It was mainly junk, but the first words of one letter caught her eye:

'ARE YOU A PREY TO NEEDLESS FEARS?'

She read on. The letter discussed 'needless fears' of an extreme kind. It referred to 'Icy Hands Gripping Your Throat', 'Shapes Lurking in Twisted Trees' and 'Ghouls Prowling at Your Back'. Its second paragraph was headed 'IS HORROR YOUR NEIGHBOUR?'

If so – and the letter aroused the gravest misgivings – you required the services of Paranoics Anonymous.

Mrs Hailstone had a soft spot for Mr Glossop, tiresome though he was, and would genuinely have liked to help him in his unusual sufferings. But she shook her head. She should know by now not to fall for postal enticements.

Yet something had to be done for him, or his hotel might go bust and with it a whole lot of jobs, including her own.

Her hand hovered over the phone.

It rang.

'Paranoics Anonymous at your service,' said a voice.

It was a man's voice, ingratiating as the voice-over in a television ad. It flowed through the channels of the ear like warm treacle.

'That was incredibly prompt!' exclaimed Mrs Hailstone.

'We like to anticipate our clients' wishes, Mrs Hailstone.'

'I'm not sure . . .' she faltered.

'Of course you're not,' said the soothing voice. 'That's why you need our services.'

'It's not for me,' said Mrs Hailstone hastily.

'Of course not,' purred the voice. 'For a friend. I quite understand.'

Mrs Hailstone made an annoyed and futile gesture.

'I don't think . . .' she began.

'Much better not, Mrs Hailstone,' said the voice. 'It disrupts tranquillity. I shall call on you tomorrow afternoon, Saturday, at 3 p.m., mingling unobtrusively with the other guests.'

'All right,' said Mrs Hailstone helplessly. 'What name shall I expect?'

'My name is Norval,' said the voice. 'Until tomorrow, goodbye, Mrs Hailstone, and rest assured you will soon say goodbye to your troubles too.'

Mrs Hailstone felt panic rising, like an innocent person in the dock who helplessly sees the evidence pointing to her guilt. She felt sure that Mr Norval had decided that 'the troubles' were her own, and that she was claiming that they were 'a friend's' because she was ashamed to admit to them. People who consulted Alcoholics Anonymous, she had heard, did this sort of thing all the time. And almost certainly, the more she protested, the less he'd believe her.

'He's probably a charlatan,' she said crossly.

Was he? She was used to seeing her name, her address, and details of her private life cunningly worked into photostat letters – which of us isn't? – but to answer a phone call before she'd even made it – that was something new.

Harriet Gardiner gazed up at the Ariel Hotel from the main street of the village of Mockery Hollow. 'Cloud capp'd towers,' she thought, vaguely recalling a line of Shakespeare's. The sun was shining after rain, and clouds of white mist wreathed the base of the noble building, so that if you stared long enough it seemed to be part of their motion, a fairy castle afloat. This impression was dispelled by her long trudge up the hill towards it, and when she looked down, the misty village itself seemed make-believe, which in a sense it was, for it was full of shops selling antiques at fantastic prices.

Within the grounds, three lawns in terraces led up to a semi-circular sweep of marble steps, at either end of which squatted a great stone lion. Inside, past the obsequious swing doors, a reverent hush fell on the ear, so that some newcomers felt inclined to genuflect or remove their shoes. The several sitting-rooms were filled with chintz-covered armchairs and silver ornaments, the walls of the lobbies were hung with expensively framed pictures, and on each landing were antique sofas and armchairs, although these, Harriet observed, were imitations. So was the George I walnut bureau in the foyer.

On the afternoon of her arrival, Harriet was examining

6

this piece of furniture when she realized that Mr Glossop was watching her. She coughed apologetically and moved away, half-expecting the proprietor to reprimand her, but he merely went on looking at her. She was used to being ogled by customers in her parents' shop – who seemed half to suppose that she too was for sale – but Mr Glossop's look was nothing like that. It was oddly apprehensive. It moved her strangely. She would have liked to pat him and say, 'There, there,' but of course a temp on her first day of a holiday job does not pat the boss.

Mavis, at the reception desk, grinned at her when Mr Glossop had gone.

'Don't worry, love. You'll get used to him.'

'He looked like a hunted fawn.'

'He always does. He's a weirdo. I called him Mr Gossip at first, until Mrs Hailstone put me right, and then when I said Glossop he looked kind of hurt and offended. I think having so much money is his trouble. I've noticed that about a lot of rich people. It brings them out in spots.'

Mavis Plimsole was already a friend, and a joy to know. She was very pretty in her way, with a slender stalk of a neck and a small round face that beamed innocent happiness so readily that it was an effort for her to look serious, and involved her forcing down the corners of her mouth. Her hair was a cluster of ginger bubbles. She spoke two languages: one a friendly Cock-ney, and the other of a 'quaite-naice' quality in which she spoke to guests. She did this with such conviction that the guests sometimes became infected and quaite-naiced her back.

'Don't tell me,' she said to Harriet when they first met, 'you're going to do Fine Arts at your university.'

'No, Mavis, biology.'

'Wrong again, Plimsole,' said Mavis, pouting. 'I've seen the way you look at the furniture, see? Sizing it up. Fake, isn't it? You know something about it, don't you?'

'Yes, a bit. My parents have got an antique shop. I've grown up with it, so it was a good guess.'

'I kid myself I'm a bit of a detective, see?' said Mavis.

The next day, Saturday, the new guests began arriving. The first through the swing doors was a tall, dark man, no longer young but of magnificent physique. He, at least, was not awestruck by the hotel's opulence. He approached the reception desk in a stately stride and gave his name in a lordly voice. It was Smith.

'Smith!' said Mavis, when he had gone. 'I bet!'

'But Mavis, why shouldn't he be Smith? It's a very common name.'

'It was the way he said it. Sort of lordly. It isn't easy to say Smith in a lordly way, but that geezer managed it. I reckon there's something fishy there.'

'Aren't you being just a bit too suspicious?'

'We'll see.'

Harriet's duties took her away from the foyer from then on, but Mavis later described the other guests in detail. (The girls had adjoining rooms on the top floor. These were not at all sumptuous. The inmates of Holloway probably enjoyed more comfort.) Mr Smith was followed by a young man named Norval. He was tall, spare, and very well-groomed. He had gentle brown eyes and dark brown hair. His voice was low and musical, too musical, too carefully modulated.

'Smooth,' said Mavis. 'Dishy, though. I wonder if he's in showbiz? Conjuror, maybe.'

Mrs Hailstone who had been watching the guests through the glass partition between the foyer and the breakfast room, came forward in a questioning way, and the two went off together.

After Mr Norval came a pair named Toothpeace. 'Toothpaste?' repeated Mavis, surprised. '*Peace, peace,*' snapped the man. 'P-e-a-c-e.' 'Mis-tah Toothpeace,' said Mavis primly. 'Doctor,' snapped the little man. 'Not a

8

doctor of medicine, you understand; a doctor of philosophy. I am the Curator of Verbal Minutiae at the British Museum.'

Mavis was at a loss. 'That's nice,' she commented lamely.

'I hardly think *nice* is appropriate in this context,' said the doctor with disdain. But his wife, surprisingly, came to Mavis's defence.

'On the contrary it is exact. "Nice" means precise, punctilious, scrupulous, particular; requiring precision, care, tact, or discrimination; delicately sensitive, discriminative, or deft.'

'It was hardly intended in that connotation,' replied her husband. 'Colloquially, it is used to mean agreeable, attractive, delightful, well-flavoured, satisfactory, kind, friendly, considerate or generally commendable.'

'I cannot concede that the young woman would describe your occupation as well-flavoured.'

The couple drifted away, bickering. Mrs Toothpeace was beautiful in a willowy, wilting fashion. She was much taller than her husband, and could have rested her chin on the top of his head, but she clearly didn't want to. 'Cat and dog, those two,' said Mavis to herself.

Guests on their own are somewhat rare in hotels, but for the third time that day one arrived. This was a Miss Hoskyn, a strapping young woman who seemed to be trying to look as unstrapping as possible. She reminded Mavis of someone badly miscast in amateur theatricals: a javelin thrower playing a fairy. 'Spoke ever so shy,' Mavis told Harriet, 'but I reckon she feels more comfortable roaring. Packs a punch, I bet.'

'Mavis, do you suspect *everyone*?'

Mavis considered. 'Yes,' she said brightly.

After the hype, the let-down. Mr Norval was younger than Mrs Hailstone had expected, and also much less self-assured. At the reception desk, he had seemed confident enough, but as he accompanied her through the hotel his composure seemed to fade. His voice rose an octave or two higher. He glanced about him with strange unease.

He tried his professional best when he faced her across her desk, but his words sounded just a little routine and lacking in conviction.

'Now, tell me all your worries and fears, Mrs Hailstone.'

'Worries?' said Mrs Hailstone briskly. 'I'm worried about Mr Glossop, my boss. Fears? I fear he's going mad.'

'I see,' said Mr Norval uncertainly.

'I'm glad you do.'

Mr Norval swallowed and blurted out the unexpected question, 'Are you still married, Mrs Hailstone?'

'Divorced. Mr Hailstone turned out to be a shower.'

'I see.'

'No, Mr Norval, you don't,' said Mrs Hailstone firmly. 'I know just what you think. You think that here's a sex-starved woman fantasizing that her boss is in love with her and palming her neurosis off on him. Mr Norval, it's nothing like that, and until you disabuse yourself of this absurd idea you're wasting your time and mine.'

'I know,' said Mr Norval meekly.

'Oh, good.'

'No, but I do, Mrs Hailstone, I really do. Look, I'll be quite honest with you: at first I did more or less think what you've just said. We get so many cases like that. We class them as "a cry for help". But I'm convinced that there is something wrong here, and you're certainly not imagining it.'

He looked quite distressed. All his strength as a counsellor seemed to have drained away. The silence became oppressive.

'Tell me,' said Mrs Hailstone, to ease the strain, 'how do you work that telephone trick?'

'No trick. I'm clairvoyant. I know what's going to happen.'

'How very convenient for you!'

'Yes, it's a gift, and very useful to my employers. But it's also a curse.'

'You foresee nasty things?'

'More often than not.'

'Is a nasty thing going to happen here?'

'It's in the air, but I can't be precise.'

'That's why you've acted so nervously since you arrived?'

'Yes.'

'Mr Norval, does this premonition of yours concern Mr Glossop?'

'I don't know as yet. Everything's blurred. I don't know why.'

'But it must be Mr Glossop. Who else could it be?' said Mrs Hailstone anxiously. She had wondered more than once if Mr Glossop's fear of women in general, which he carried to a ludicrous extent, might mask a genuine fear of some particular woman, out to get him. Someone scorned, like whom hell had no fury?

'But just what nasty thing is in the air, Mr Norval?'

'I'm not sure.'

'Yes you are,' said Mrs Hailstone, eyeing him closely. 'I know you are. Tell me.'

'I'd rather not.'

'I insist that you do.'

'Oh all right,' said Mr Norval gloomily. 'Murder.'

2

That same evening Harriet was working in the bar. The first person to enter it was Mr Smith. He advanced to the counter with slow, pantherish steps, like a general to the gate of a conquered city. Sheer power vibrated from him. If he could have been fitted with a socket his energy, plugged in, would have been enough to light the hotel or operate its lifts. Harriet, however, was not impressed. For all she cared, he could have been a rhinoceros in the zoo.

He remained standing at the bar, sipping his drink, and one or two couples came in and were served. Then in came Mrs Hubert Toothpeace by herself. She managed to look, thought Harriet, as if she were swooning while walking along. She swayed towards the counter, and a man who was standing between her and Mr Smith collected his drinks and carried them to a table, so that she beheld Mr Smith in full view. She now swooned in earnest. She uttered a weak moan and her body gave way gracefully at every joint in turn, beginning at her ankles and concluding at her neck, and she slid to the floor and lay there white and limp.

For all his vibrating power, etc., Mr Smith was not quick to react. He was like a great ship trying to turn in a small harbour. Harriet was kneeling beside Mrs Tooth-peace, and the two couples at the tables had wandered over doubtfully, looking rather offended, before Mr

Smith had done more than bend at the waist. Harriet raised Mrs Toothpeace to a sitting position and pushed her head towards her knees, but she flopped like a rag doll, and Harriet looked up anxiously at the others.

'There's a First Aid room next to this bar – '

'Lead me to it,' said Mr Smith dramatically. He gathered up Mrs Toothpeace as easily as if she had been a bag of straw, and the males of the two couples, one of whom had a hernia and the other a slipped disc, looked relieved and with appropriate murmurs of concern returned to their tables.

'I ought to get back to the bar, sir,' said Harriet, as Mr Smith laid Mrs Toothpeace on a couch. 'I'll ring Reception and get them to fetch her husband.'

'Her husband,' said Mr Smith. 'Ha!'

Harriet looked at him rather impatiently. He was distinctly slow on the uptake. He was about as prompt as the stone lions out front.

'Could you stay with her for a minute, sir?' She hurried back to the bar, where several new arrivals were stamping their feet and looking impatiently about for the barmaid.

Mr Smith, after a look round, said in a commanding tone, 'Angela, pull yourself together!'

'Oh John,' said Mrs Toothpeace faintly.

'This will never do,' said Mr Smith. 'Such weak behaviour will betray us.'

'I know,' said Angela Toothpeace penitently. 'It is most self-sacrificing of you, John, to give up your position as Governor of the Bank of England just to devote yourself to me.' She worked herself feebly into a sitting position. 'It was the shock of seeing you that overcame me. And the knowledge that you have come here to kill my husband.'

'I am the slave of my own will,' said Mr Smith sombrely. 'It was this that drove me, at the age of eighteen, to win the Nobel prize for Chemistry, and at nineteen to become the Heavyweight Champion of the World. All that lies in my path, I must sweep aside.'

'Like Hubert.'

'Like Hubert.'

'Must we kill him, John?'

'What honourable alternative is there? Adultery is immoral. Bigamy is a crime.'

'Yet it does seem a pity.'

'Pity is a word that we must erase from our vocabulary. All's fair in love and war, and this is love, fundamental love.'

'Ah,' sighed Angela, 'that is a word I have never heard Hubert use.'

'Love?'

'No, *fundamental*,' replied Angela. 'He prefers *basic*.' She frowned. 'Erase from our vocabulary . . . ?'

'Ah, Angela,' cut in Mr Smith impatiently, 'why on earth did you marry him?'

'Well, it was such a promising marriage at first. He'd just got his job as curator, and I was one of a team compiling the latest thesaurus. It seemed a perfect match. But before long Hubert became deliberately perverse. He challenged everything I said. We quarrelled dreadfully once, over the definition of a fireplace. I said that the grate was an *orifice*. Which,' added Angela vexedly, 'it obviously *is*. Hubert insisted on *egress*, which is quite ridiculous. We wrangled about it vehemently. At last he stepped into the grate, shouting, "I'll *prove* it's an egress!" and climbed into the chimney.'

'And came out on the roof?' asked Mr Smith, interested in spite of himself.

'No,' said Angela contemptuously. 'He just crawled back, covered with soot.'

'Yes, well,' said Mr Smith, 'to this matter of his extermination – '

14

'I think perhaps *extirpation* has the finer shade of meaning,' said Angela.

'Whatever you like. I have already made several suggestions . . .'

'Which,' said Angela, with unexpected firmness, 'are really out of the question. I cannot agree to your chopping Hubert up into little pieces and dispersing him among litter bins and left-luggage offices. Neither could I acquiesce in your dissolving him in rapidly-acting chemicals and selling him as garden compost.'

'My propositions,' said Mr Smith huffily, 'were practical, positive. They had point, purpose. Your rejections are deleterious, destructive.'

'I don't care, care,' said Angela, quite petulantly. 'You must think of something else . . .' She rose shakily to her feet. 'Didn't that girl say she was sending for Hubert? He's a long time coming . . .'

As soon as his wife had left their hotel bedroom, Hubert Toothpeace had slipped into the corridor and made his way to the third door on the left. Before he could knock it opened, and the hand of Miss Hoskyn shot through it and lugged him into the room.

'What-ho, Hubie, me ole fruit!' she yelled in a trenchant county accent, clumping him on the back. 'You've got rid of old Anaemic Annie, then?'

'Yes, indeed, Amanda,' said Hubert, giggling happily. 'I pretended to be searching under the dressing table for an adverbial particle. Wasn't that – ' – he pronounced the words deliberately and delightedly, ' – a "spiffing wheeze"?'

'That's subtle, Hube,' said Miss Hoskyn, clumping him again. 'Give us a kiss!'

'Darling,' said Hubert, as she gave him a kiss like a boxer's left jab, 'how wonderful of you to give up your stately home and the title of Duchess of Sligo to live like a commoner, all for the love of me! Oh, it is so good to have you, someone with whom I can relax and abandon the rigid pedantry which is the curse of my occupation.' He chuckled. 'Did you hear me say "spiffing wheeze" just now?' He became suddenly anxious. 'You don't think "corking jape", perhaps? No, no,' he added quickly, 'that wouldn't apply: *wheeze* signifies plan, scheme, while *jape* suggests jest, act of buffoonery . . . *Corking wheeze* would be admissible . . .'

'Let's get down to brass tacks, though, old sport,' said the Duchess. 'We've got to get rid of old Emotional Neurasthenia, and the sooner the better.'

'Yet . . . actual murder does seem somewhat drastic . . .'

'Yes, and more than a little decisive. Ah, come on, she's death warmed up already; what's a little *rigor mortis*?'

'Won't there be . . . difficulties?' asked Hubert apprehensively.

'We must ride roughshod over 'em, Hube. Pity your wife doesn't hunt. Then we could ride roughshod over *her*. Nothin' like a hunt to make murder look natural. Why on earth did you marry her, Hube?'

'Well, it was such a promising marriage at first. I'd just got my job as curator and she was at work on the thesaurus. We used to sit by the fire, doing crosswords or playing Lexicon. But one word led to another. It was, "Is the kettle boiling?" "No, dear, but the water in it is." You see? The sarcastic inference? In such exchanges are hidden the small daggers of incompatibility.'

'Don't follow you, Hube, but daggers are out. Too messy.'

'We took to watching each other for a slip in grammar or a misused term,' went on Hubert. 'Like snipers behind cover, each waiting for the other to let fall a solecism.'

'We might fake a car crash . . .' said the Duchess. 'No, too dicey.'

'The quarrels we had over the misuse of the word

"hopefully"'!' said Hubert. 'The tantrums over split infinitives!'

'I'm a good shot, mind you,' said the Duchess. 'But fakin' a gun-suicide is dodgy. Angle of entry of bullet, and all that.'

'Misrelated participles – they were a source of strife!'

'Hubert! You're not listenin'!'

'Oh yes I am,' said Hubert. 'You have employed some refreshing colloquialisms: *fake, dodgy, dicey* . . . They lent gusto to an otherwise macabre deliberation . . .'

'Hubert! How shall we do her in?'

'No, no – "do her in" is a vile phrase . . .'

'Wait a bit. Someone's comin'.'

It was Mavis, who, unable to find anyone to look for Hubert, was doing so herself. Hubert incautiously opened the door to peep out, and she accosted him.

'Doctor Toothpeace, your wife has fainted, sir. Will you come quickly?'

Hubert went after her meekly enough, and the Duchess became Miss Hoskyn, pretending to read a magazine. Goodness knew who she thought she was fooling, but it was not Mavis, who had taken in the scene, her face a blank and her eye as bright as a blackbird's.

Hubert followed Mavis into the First Aid Room, and Mr Smith took his leave. He could not resist a contemptuous backward glance.

'Ha!'

'Ha?' said Hubert. 'Yes, I can accept ha. A kind of staccato laughter. Now, Angela my dear: it seems that you are indisposed . . .'

The Duchess of Sligo threw down her magazine and sprang up.

'Oh dammit,' she exclaimed, 'this is gettin' us nowhere. Let's think. I'm cleanin' gun – gun goes off. Old Creepin' Paralysis gets in the way – blows her in two –

sheer accident – blame no one. Yes, I like that. It's simple and straightforward. Minor problem – how can I get her to stand in the way when I'm cleanin' gun? – Never mind – that'll sort itself out . . .'

As a planned murder it would not have won any prizes, but the Duchess had the aristocrat's fine disdain for vulgar practicalities. She pulled a black leather jacket over her magnificent shoulders and produced an expensive shot-gun from the wardrobe.

'Better practise a bit,' she said. 'Accident's got to look natural.'

She intended to 'practise' in a nearby wood, but as she entered the corridor she encountered Mr Glossop, who in his role of proprietor was dutifully patrolling the hotel. Although short and fat, he was managing to look important, until he saw the Duchess, who swung out upon him as if from an ambush, her gun pointing at his stomach. He gave a strangulated cry, stumbled, and knocked a blue basalt copy of the Portland Vase off a French marquetry jardinière. The vase survived its fall on the soft carpet, but not the heel of Mr Glossop, who trod on it as he recovered himself and snapped off one of its handles. He leaned against the wall, his eyes bolting; then with an heroic effort he straightened, and with a sickly smile continued his parade. After he had turned the corner, however, the Duchess heard the panicky scamper of his feet on the stairs.

'Extraordinary feller,' she remarked to herself, and strode on.

'I tell you, Harriet, he was in Hoskyn's room!'

'There must be some explanation.'

'You bet there's an explanation. Don't tell me he'd dropped in to borrow some sugar!'

'But Mavis, it's impossible!'

'When you've been in this world as long as I have,

18

dear,' said Mavis, who was twenty, 'you'll know nothing's impossible where *that's* concerned.'

'She could run about with him in her jaws!'

'Well, maybe that's how they like it. I said that that Hoskyn was a funny one, didn't I?'

'This is a funny place altogether,' said Harriet.

'You reckon?'

'Yes,' said Harriet. She thought of her first view of the hotel when it had seemed to be floating in the clouds. 'It's . . . there's something unreal about it.'

'Good place for a murder, maybe,' said Mavis, her pretty face lighting up.

At the rear of the Ariel Hotel's farthest lawn, facing the hotel, was a 'niche house', yellow-white and overgrown with ivy, with two portals. In the left-hand portal stood a statue of St Phocas, the patron saint of gardeners, in Roman robes. His gaze was steadily averted from the right-hand portal, where stood a marble lady in a great quantity of draperies that had slipped down to her hips, at which she was gazing with modest complacency. Mr Smith glanced moodily and absently at it as he slouched through the grass the next morning.

For the first time in his overwhelming career he was baffled. He knew a great deal about the world, but the world he knew a great deal about was male. The female world disconcerted him. How could he ruthlessly sweep aside all that lay in his path if Angela Toothpeace kept standing in his way? He had suggested every known means of assassination and she had continually demurred, as if she were buying a dress.

Behind the niche house was the Ariel's private wood, covering the slope that led down to the village. Mr Smith made his smouldering way into it. A loud report near to his right startled him, and parting the bushes, he came upon Miss Hoskyn, seated on a fallen tree trunk. A wisp of smoke wafted from the barrel of her gun.

'Good morning,' he said stiffly.

'Hi,' said the Duchess. She peered at him with increased interest. 'Wait a minute. I've seen you somewhere before. Smith? That name doesn't sound right. Didn't you swim the Channel a year or two back?'

'Fully-clothed. For a bet,' admitted Mr Smith good-naturedly.

'That's it,' said the Duchess, snapping her fingers. 'Saw you in the papers. You're Sir John Marvell, aren't you?'

'The same,' said Sir John. His eyes lit up. 'And I've seen *you* before, too. You're not Miss Hoskyn. You're the Duchess of Sligo. I saw you in the *Tatler*. Showing your race card to a friend.'

'To a twit who broke his neck at the next meet, actually. But you're right, that's me. Just what are you doin' here, Sir John, demeanin' yourself as Smith?'

'I might ask the same of you.'

'Ah, point taken. Oh dammit, we'd better both come clean, what? Look, this is it. I'm here to bump off this wiltin' daffodil, this what's-a-name – Angela Tooth-peace. I plan to marry her husband, Hubert.'

'Then this,' said Sir John, exhaling a heavy breath, 'is quite a coincidence.'

'What? You mean you . . . Do I get this right, Sir John? You plan to kill Hubert? Good God. But not to . . . Surely not to marry that languishin' lily? . . . Well, what do you know? Oh well, no offence, everyone to his taste . . . But look here, now that we know how we stand, can't we just take them off each other's hands?'

Sir John stood a moment in thought, concentrating so hard that the air around him quivered slightly. He sat beside her on the tree trunk. 'No, we couldn't,' he said sombrely. 'We've got our social positions to consider.'

'Point taken,' said the Duchess ruefully. 'I see your meanin'. I couldn't turn up to a hunt meet in the company of a divorcee. They're very hot about that sort of thing.'

'And in my position,' said Sir John, 'I could not keep a mistress.'

They stared at each other in perplexity.

'Dashed awkward,' said the Duchess.

'Very.'

'So what does one do now?'

Their conversation was interrupted by the appearance of Mr Norval. He was groping his way along as if he were blindfolded. As he neared the pair he veered towards them like a child getting 'warmer' in a party game. He stumbled through the bushes and into their little clearing. He stood still, seemed to wake up, nodded a greeting, and went on.

'Do you think he heard us?' murmured Sir John.

'Never mind him.'

The hearty Duchess and the dynamic Sir John pondered their problem in a moody silence.

'Oh dammit,' exclaimed the Duchess at last, 'we're both good sports, aren't we? What say we make a sportin' contest of this, Sir John, ten grand a side?'

'I don't follow you.'

'Look, either you kill Hubert or I kill Angela, and whoever gets there first takes the money and the game's over. It makes the thing more excitin', what? Just bein' Hoskyn, havin' to keep puttin' g's on the end of words, is so borin', and I want to get rid of Hoskyn as soon as poss.'

'I never could resist a bet,' conceded Sir John.

'Great! and may the better man win!' She grabbed his hand and pumped it. 'And what say we compare notes as we go along?'

'Wait, now. You actually propose that we discuss our plans with each other?'

'Well, why not? It'd make it all the more sportin'.'

'But wouldn't that defeat our object?'

'I always say, it's not winnin' or losin' that counts, it's the game.'

'I like your style, Duchess,' said Sir John. 'Besides, by helping each other we shall be aiding our own victims, and that makes it moral. I agree to the plan.'

They shook hands and went companionably back to the hotel.

3

One of Harriet's duties was to make the beds and tidy up the rooms when the guests had vacated them for the morning. Naturally, she had to do this with discretion, but it was generally assumed that everyone would get out by ten o'clock, and from then on until lunch time the hotel would be all but empty of visitors.

The exception was Mr Norval, who sauntered in and out of the sitting-rooms and up and down the corridors, looking at the false antiques, or rather not looking at them, but looking about him as if searching for something, and sometimes even gazing up into the air, as though inspiration was to be found in the ceiling. He reminded Harriet of the Dong with the Luminous Nose on his mournful quest for the Jumbly Girl, and she felt quite desolate for him.

This morning she ventured into his room, supposed at first sight that it was empty, and began tidying up. On turning, however, she came upon him stretched out on his bed. She said, 'Oh, I beg your pardon,' and hastily picked up her cleaning things; but he spoke:

'St Phocas . . .'

Harriet was not sure whether this required an answer.

'I beg your pardon, sir?'

'. . . Phocas . . .'

'Focus?' repeated Harriet, excusably confused.

'St Phocas and the marble woman . . .'

He was asleep, she decided. She moved just a little nearer. His eyes were open, but glassy, and he looked crumpled with tiredness. He aroused her maternal instincts. 'There now,' she said, meaninglessly.

'Beware the marble woman . . .'

'Yes, I will. Don't worry, now.'

'Beware St Phocas . . .'

'Yes, him too. Sh'sh . . .'

But Mr Norval woke up with a start and swung his legs to the floor. Harriet backed away instinctively, although she knew he was not dangerous; whenever he happened upon her tidying up he would put a careful distance between them, apologetic, as if he were the intruder. 'Oh dear,' he said, 'was I talking in my sleep?'

'A bit. Why don't you lie down again, sir? You do look tired.'

'Talking nonsense, was I?'

'You were just dreaming.'

'No, actually,' said Mr Norval, in a wearily matter-of-fact way, '*this* is the dream. What sounded like nonsense was real.'

Harriet was a practical person, scientifically inclined, and as a rule she treated mystic utterances of this kind with impatience. She accepted that there were more things in heaven and earth, etc., but she felt more comfortable in the area of reason and common sense. Yet there was a peculiar sincerity about Mr Norval that she could not dismiss. She knew enough about young men to know that they could resort to the most extraordinary tricks to gain their unvarying ends, but she thought she knew enough about Mr Norval to know that he was not guilty of any ulterior motive. She said with assumed cheerfulness, 'I'm afraid that's beyond me,' but he had actually fallen asleep again, his legs still trailing on the floor. For a moment she looked at him, defenceless in sleep, and hesitated as to whether to lift up his legs and straighten him on to the bed; but she thought better of it and left the room, casting a doubtful, even rather irritated glance at him as she went.

She pushed Mavis's door open with her foot and entered her room carrying a mug of cocoa in each hand. She sat on the edge of the bed and drew her dressing-gown about her. 'Mr Norval – ' she began.

'Oo yes, dishy,' said Mavis.

'He's weird.'

'Dishy, though.'

'Weird,' said Harriet, more severely than she felt, because she did not want to betray any softer feelings for Mr Norval. 'He talks in riddles.'

Mavis dabbed cocoa from her lips with a tissue. 'You know what I think?' she said. 'I think he's a private detective.'

'Why?'

'It's the way he snoops around, peering at everything as if he was looking for fingerprints. He never leaves the hotel – he's here on business! Or actually,' said Mavis, 'he does go out – just into the grounds – and you know what? He's following that Hoskyn! He's trailing her! And it may be,' added Mavis, frowning, 'that he's trailing Smith as well. I've seen that Smith around with Hoskyn. I bet they're plotting something.'

'Suspicions!' said Harriet.

'All right, next time you do his room, look out for a magnifying glass or a finger print outfit. I still maintain he's dishy.'

'Loopy,' said Harriet adamantly.

'Well, maybe he is, it wouldn't make me wrong about him.'

'No?'

'No. I've read hundreds of detective stories and they come in all kinds – posh detectives, scruffy detectives, priest detectives, old maid detectives, foreign detectives, drunk detectives, blind detectives – you name it. I've never yet come across a mad detective, but maybe he's it.'

'Well,' conceded Harriet, 'private detectives suss out marriage partners who are having affairs, don't they? Do you think Mr Norval is in the employ of Mrs Tooth-peace?'

'That would be rather boring,' said Mavis. 'I'd sooner it was a murder.'

Mrs Hailstone, always kind and encouraging to Harriet, enlightened her as to how St Phocas spelt his name and where he and 'the marble woman' were to be found.

'Why do you ask, Harriet?'

'I just wondered. I heard the name somewhere.'

She still could not imagine why the two statues should trouble the dreams of Mr Norval, and so she was left wondering.

The Ariel bar was open to the public, and at six o'clock every evening it would fill with people who, having been swindled in the antique shops in the village, would gladly buy drinks at exorbitant prices in the belief that this was gracious living. It happened this evening that Harriet and Mavis were working here together. Mavis murmured, 'See that man in the corner?'

'You mean,' said Harriet, 'the one with the sand cord jacket with paisley lining, co-ordinating paisley waist-coat, button-down chambray shirt with (probably) two front pockets, and matching cord trousers?'

'Yes. Look at his shoes.'

Harriet did so on the pretext of fetching up a crate of tonic water from under the counter. 'Oh no!' she exclaimed. 'Black!'

The shoes were indeed black, square-toed, and laced. 'He ran out of cash before he reached his feet?' suggested Harriet.

'My guess is that he got that outfit from a dress-hire

shop,' said Mavis. 'Bit sad, isn't it? He'll have to give it back like Cinderella. Only he forgot the glass slippers. You know what I think? He's a cop. He's a cop in mufti.'

'You've got cops on the brain, Mavis.'

'We'll see. Oho, what have we here?'

Here we had Mr Norval, who bought a tomato juice and took this harmless drink among the tables, looking about him in his usual questing fashion.

'Now watch,' whispered Mavis. 'I bet he goes to him.'

Mr Norval went right up to the table of the well-dressed young man with the incongruous shoes. Mavis's nice face was aglow with anticipation. But he moved on and sat elsewhere.

'Not in league,' said Harriet.

'They could have exchanged a secret message.'

'Go on with you.'

'I bet he's a cop anyway,' said Mavis obstinately.

The bar was now crowded with customers and further discussion was out of the question. Hours later, however, in Harriet's room, (Mavis's turn to make the cocoa), they eagerly pursued the matter.

'The police and the private detective work together in lots of detective stories,' said Mavis.

'There's a lot wrong with your theories, Mavis. I can't see a woman calling in a private detective *and* the police to chase up her husband's infidelities. And if Doctor Toothpeace really is having it off with Miss Hoskyn, would he actually bring his wife to the same hotel? And where does Mr Smith fit in?'

'Yes, it gets curiouser and curiouser, doesn't it?' said Mavis happily. 'Perhaps it's not just a matter of chasing up infidelities. Perhaps there really is going to be a murder. That would be lovely.'

'Mavis, how could you be so wicked?'

'Oh, I don't want anyone to get hurt. What I would like,' said Mavis wistfully, 'would be a murder that didn't really *matter*. That would be lovely.'

'I think any murder has its serious side,' said Harriet.

'I've always loved detective stories,' said Mavis, 'but only the country house kind – you know, the kind where Sir Giles is found dead in the library by a maid who screams and everyone is under suspicion and the least likely one is the murderer and is found out by monocled Lord Percy who everyone thinks is a twit but turns out to be a super-sleuth. I don't like the ones where the private eye is beaten up by thugs in an alley every two pages. I like a nice cosy murder. This hotel is just right for one of those.'

Mavis was again at work at the reception desk the next morning, and who should turn up asking for a single room but the well-dressed young man with the ill-matched shoes, only now he was wearing a classic green single-breasted tweed jacket with double vents, a wine twill shirt, and ginger sportsman cord trousers. Mavis, agog with interest, and quaite-naicing him breathlessly, managed to peep at his feet. He was wearing penny loafers in tan leather and perfect taste. Someone had tipped him off about the shoes.

'Neem please?' said Mavis.

'PC Mogpuss,' said the young man, and then clapped a hand to his mouth. He had let out the 'PC' involuntarily. Mavis, inwardly overjoyed, dealt with this with ready tact.

'Er – how do you spell "Peacey", sir?' she asked. 'You do write it with a hyphen, I suppose, sir?'

Sir looked relieved and grateful. 'Oh, leave it out,' he said. 'Just put W. Mogpuss. Yes, actually, I am – er – Peacey hyphen Mogpuss, but I don't care about using a double-barrelled name.'

'More at home with a double-barrelled shot gun,' remarked Mavis to herself gleefully. And later, to Harriet: 'So what about that, sweetie? The plot thickens, eh? I bet you a murder has been arranged!'

4

'I tell you she levelled a gun at me,' Mr Glossop had said, his eyes bulging.

Mrs Hailstone was frankly quite concerned at this, but it was essential not to show it.

'I'm sure she didn't, Mr Glossop. I'm sure she was just *carrying* a gun, which is quite natural.'

'*Natural!*'

'Certainly. The people who come to this hotel are mostly collectors, aren't they? It's fashionable to collect weapons. What kind of gun was it? A blunderbuss? An Elizabethan flintlock with powder-horn, perhaps?'

'I didn't notice,' muttered Mr Glossop.

'Well, there you are!' (Mrs Hailstone had banked on this. The mere sight of this Amazon would have blinded him to details.) 'A harmless collector!'

She summoned up every facial muscle to give him a reassuring smile. It did have some effect. He turned up his coat collar, put on his dark glasses, and crept out. Mrs Hailstone's smile sagged.

'M'm,' she said. 'Better phone the police.'

'If someone's toting a gun in your place, Iris,' said the Superintendent, who knew Mrs Hailstone well, 'I'd better have a word with her.'

'Thank you, Cyril, but softly softly please. This is the high season for the Ariel, and if the guests got the idea that there was a terrorist in their midst they'd cancel their bookings and cost us the earth. And as I've explained, we may have got it all wrong.'

'Yes, sure, but we'd better keep an eye on her. I'll slip an officer into the hotel. I'll send PC Mogpuss. He's a conscientious lad, if a bit thick.'

'Fine. Have him come by the bar this evening, and we'll fix him up with a room tomorrow.'

'Yes, good idea. One thing, though. He'll have to be in plain clothes, of course, and I doubt if his wardrobe comes up to your posh standards.'

'Don't worry about that, Cyril. I'll see that he gets all the clothes he needs.'

Harriet, in spite of herself, was getting more and more interested in Mr Norval. In spite of herself because, for one thing, too great an interest might affect her friendship with Mavis, who had also taken a fancy to the young man and his brooding good looks. For another, she feared that he really was mad, and for all the assurances by the surrealists that madness was a desirable state, she thought it best avoided.

She had discovered that his first name was Norman. Norman Norval. She felt that this had some special significance, but she could not possibly say why.

She took to tidying up his room for longer periods than was strictly necessary. It was noticeable that he always happened to come in while she was doing so. He would glance at her with his gentle brown eyes and then studiously glance away. She would busy herself with her work, taking no notice. An atmosphere was building up between them.

Perhaps this narrative has not said enough about Harriet's looks. She could have appeared with credit on one of the holier Christmas cards. In certain lights she could be mistaken for an angel, and men who saw her then would resolve to lead purer lives. She was not vain, but she did sometimes use her looks to her advantage. As a result, Mr Norval's glances were beginning to suggest a forlorn devotion.

It was sad that he seemed so sad.

This morning he said suddenly, 'Do you like the poems of Ted Hughes?'

'Very much.'

'Do you know, I usually know what he's going to write? I could write some of his poems days before he's thought them out and forestall him if I wanted to.'

Alas, he was mad. 'That would be cheating,' said Harriet gently.

'Of course it would,' said Mr Norval bleakly.

Harriet put aside her duster and sat on the dressing-table stool. 'Mr Norval,' she said, 'I can't help noticing that you seem worried. Excuse my asking, but what is it?'

'Success.'

'And that worries you? Most people are afraid of the opposite! Can you really foretell the future?'

He nodded glumly.

'Why, you must be the envy of everyone!'

'Fools,' said Mr Norval. 'Have you ever read Virgil's *Aeneid*, Harriet?'

'Er, no.'

'There's a character in it named Cassandra. She could foretell the future too. Much good did it do her. She foretold the fall of Troy. They just said she was mad, which made her madder still.'

'But that's different. Why should you fear success?'

'It's the way I could get it. As you say, cheating. There's always a comeback when you cheat. You don't get away with it.'

'M'm,' said Harriet. She saw the sense of that. She approved. But she looked at him with feelings mixed of doubt and pity.

'You don't believe it, do you?' he said. 'All right, I'll

31

show you.' He picked up a newspaper and opened it at the racing page. 'Here, name a race.'

Harriet peered at the unfamiliar columns. 'The one-forty-five Malton Selling Stakes,' she read out uncertainly.

'Saldivar,' said Mr Norval without hesitation. 'Check it in the evening paper. *But*,' he added urgently, 'you won't back it, will you? On no account back it.'

'I wouldn't know how,' Harriet assured him.

'Well, don't find out. You'd win, but it wouldn't be worth it. That sort of good luck always brings bad luck after it.'

'All right.'

She had stayed too long, and had to leave. She went into the next room and tidied up absent-mindedly. She understood what he meant by cheating; she realized how frustrated he must be; but if what he said was true, surely he had a tremendous gift for doing good? What about preventing disasters, etc.? She felt suddenly vexed with him. 'He's mad,' she said yet again, crossly. Yes: but perhaps only mad north-north-west?

Mr Glossop had an office on the third floor, in the strip of corridor past the door marked '*Private, Staff Only*'. Harriet was not allowed into his office, but every morning she was required to collect and empty his wastepaper basket, which he left outside his door.

She took it to the chute and had tipped it half over when a sheet of paper caught her eye. It was covered with names. Just names, like signatures, but all in one hand.

After a look round she fished it out, straightened it, and read:

Dominic Deverell. This was written at least twenty times, in large bold handwriting with flourishes.

Roderick Richelieu. Ditto.

Galahad Gastonbury. He hadn't been too sure of this one. The 'Gs' were sprawly, like bad Ss.

Franklin Fortescue . . .
Hannibal Harbinger . . .

Harriet was a better detective than the observant Mavis. She saw more deeply into things. She began where Mavis left off.

She remembered Mavis's saying that she had called the proprietor 'Mr Gossip', and that when she had corrected it to Glossop it had somehow managed to upset him. She remembered her first sight of him, and his startling reappearance in dark glasses. Disguise?

She looked at the names on the list. They were multi-syllabled and resonant, such as might appear in romantic historical novels. He had written them with the most extravagant dashes and curls.

She put two and two together. He was not on good terms with himself. He wanted to look and sound like someone else.

This was sad.

PC Mogpuss, wearing a navy-with-wine-pinstripe double-breasted suit with plain back and jetted pockets, a wine stripe double-cuff shirt and a grape-design silk tie, and looking as if he had stepped out of a West End tailor's catalogue, or rather had stepped into it by mistake, picked up the phone in his room and looked at it like an alerted tracker-dog. He had the look of a good Boy Scout who takes every point of the Scout Law very seriously.

'Sarge? Mogpuss. I've got this woman under surveillance. A Miss Hoskyn. Speaks timidly, but from her accent I think she may be Irish.'

'Irish, eh?' came the voice of the sergeant. 'Well, try to confirm that suspicious and incriminating fact, Officer. See if she lets slip any Irish expressions. For your guidance, such expressions might be begorrah, bejabers, bedad, gossoon, spalpeen, mavourneen, and shillelagh.'

'Very good, Sarge,' said PC Mogpuss. 'I am obeying orders, I am observing this woman, but I will not prejudge her. So far she has done nothing to arouse my suspicion. It's even possible that she's being intimidated. Her quiet voice doesn't seem natural to me.'

'Yes, all right, but just keep an eye on her, that's what you're there for, all togged up. Have you ever been to Ireland?'

'No, but I've seen plays on telly about it, and they've given me a pretty good idea. Trust me, I'll get into conversation with her and bring the subject up, discreetly. For instance, I might say something about black-haired colleens in red petticoats tickling trout in the boreens.'

'In the *what*?'

'Boreens.'

'You'd look a right idiot if you said that. A boreen is a path.'

'Oh.'

'I should let her use the Irish expressions if I were you. Now do your duty.'

'Willco.'

It was Harriet's afternoon off, and she was on her way to her parents in the village. On an impulse she crossed the lowest lawn and went to the niche house to examine St Phocas and his half-dressed companion. At close range the statues lost some of their classical grace and dignity. They were splashed with bird lime and plastered with leaves and lightly coated with a curious scum, as if someone had dusted them with grubby flour. Harriet entered the niche house and found that the two portals led into a single room about six feet square, with a musty smell suggestive of the tomb, but in spite of that she could see nothing to 'beware of' in the statues, which were surely the passive butts of wind, rain and the birds – unless, of course, they fell on you. Prompted by this idea, she got behind St Phocas, placed her hands on his back and pushed. He was about her own height and extremely heavy, quite beyond her power to move him, but she could see he was not fixed to the plinth.

A gardener appeared outside the niche house, pushing a wheelbarrow. Harriet was just about to step out with assumed coolness when Miss Hoskyn came up to him in a bouncing, swinging stride that threatened the mowing down of all who stood in her path. Oh, surely Mavis was right: that quiet voice of hers couldn't be her normal one. Any doubts were dispelled when she said in strident tones, 'Fetch me a packet of weedkiller, my man.'

The gardener was very old, ninety-seven at least, and gnarled and wizened and misanthropic. He eyed Miss Hoskyn balefully. He croaked, 'What for?'

'To kill weeds. Be quick.'

'You got weeds in your room? First I heard of weeds in a hotel room.'

'What business is that of yours, you old goat? Do as you're told and don't babble.'

'I ain't giving you no weedkiller. Get it in the village.'

Harriet now feared that Miss Hoskyn might trample the old man underfoot, but at that very moment PC Mogpuss came up, wearing a single-breasted rust jacket, lovat-green pleat-front trousers with turn-ups, a cool blue button-down shirt and an abstract floral wool tie. He said in a commanding voice, 'What reason have you for refusing that perfectly civil request, gardener?'

'I ain't giving no one no weedkiller. I ain't giving no one nothing.'

'I have reason to believe,' said Wilfred Mogpuss, 'that if a man had asked you you would have complied at once. Because you have a defenceless woman to deal with' – he glanced from the decrepit nonagenarian to Miss Hoskyn's powerful frame – 'you think you can take advantage of her. Give her what she asks at once.'

'I ain't giving no one – '

'Perhaps this will persuade you.'

Harriet craned as much as she dared. She could not see what 'this' was, but she could guess. Goodness! A policeman's identity card! He was a cop after all!

'Can't read without me glasses,' said the gardener.

'Police.'

(There you are, then!)

'If she wants it she can fetch it herself,' grumbled the gardener, and pointed with a claw-like hand to a shed a dozen yards away.

Miss Hoskyn strode back in triumph bearing a packet boldly labelled 'weedkiller', and unreservedly became the Duchess of Sligo. So exultant was she that she lost all restraint and broke into rich county idiom.

'Well done, lad! 'Pon my word, I like your style!' She gave Wilfred Mogpuss a clump on the back that staggered him, strongly made though he was. 'Anythin' I can ever do for you, be sure to ask me, what?' She glanced approvingly at his brand new, finest quality clothes. 'We members of the upper classes must stick together, eh?' She turned to the gardener and spoke with the same high good humour. 'No hard feelin's, old feller. You lost that round, but never mind, you stood up for yourself. I like that!' And she clumped him as well, sending him head first into the leaves in his wheelbarrow.

Wilfred Mogpuss's face filled with quiet pride. So might a devoted teacher have looked when he had succeeded in making a backward child read its first words. Miss Hoskyn beamed, clumped him again, said, 'Good huntin', what?' and strode away. After taking three or four strides she stopped, remembered that she had taken it upon herself to speak quietly, and came back with little mincing steps.

'Thank you so much,' she said in a tiny voice.

Harriet meanwhile managed to slip out of the niche house and was on her way, but PC Mogpuss caught up with her.

'You work in the hotel, I believe, madam?'

'That's right.'

'Are you downtrodden, madam?'

'Not a bit,' said Harriet cheerfully.

'Because you have your rights, madam, and no one should ignore the fact.'

'Well, if anyone downtreads me, I'll let you know.'

'Good, madam. You will always have a friend in me. Did you hear me speaking to that lady?'

'Well, yes.'

'Then you must have noticed what a difference it made, my standing up for her? You must have heard the way she speaks normally, poor cowed creature?'

'She was speaking up pretty well before you intervened,' said Harriet.

'Yes, raising her voice to keep her courage up, poor thing.'

'Why do you think she wants weedkiller?' said Harriet.

'She may keep a window box.'

'And takes it round with her on a lead,' thought Harriet. She said goodbye and went on her way to the village, longing all the while to get her visit over and tell Mavis the news.

Passing a newsagent's, she remembered the Malton Selling Stakes and bought an early edition evening paper.

One-forty-five: (1) Saldivar (2) Megan's Realm (3) Argie-Bargie.

'Well, well,' she said.

'I have kept Miss Hoskyn under close surveillance, Sergeant,' said PC Mogpuss into the phone, 'and I am more convinced than ever of her innocence. Her gun is licensed, and I have no doubt she uses it solely for harmless purposes like shooting birds and animals.'

'Still, if she's Irish – ' said the sergeant doubtfully.

37

'I am not even sure of that. I have not heard her use any expressions such as alanna, acushla, or top o' the mornin' to ye. She has in fact an aristocratic mode of speech. She mentioned to me that she belonged to the upper classes. That does put a different complexion on it, doesn't it? I mean, the Force exists to protect the upper classes, not to pry into their affairs.'

'In that case, officer, you'd better drop the case and come back to the station.'

'One minute, Sergeant,' said PC Mogpuss. He was wearing a navy-blue melton blouson with tan trim, which he much preferred to his uniform. 'She still needs keeping an eye on. She often speaks in a crushed manner and I have reason to believe that she may be intimidated. She is much in the company of a hulking brute here named Smith, and I think he may have some hold over her.'

'Oh, keep an eye on him, then,' said the sergeant reluctantly.

'Willco.'

5

Sir John Marvell and the Duchess of Sligo sat side by side in the wood, engaged in pleasant discourse. Their arrogant natures cancelled each other out, so that, affably discussing murder together, they both became nicer persons.

'I admire your forthright style, Duchess,' said Sir John, 'but don't you think that asking the gardener outright for weedkiller was just a little *too* open?'

'I don't believe in beatin' about the bush.'

'How will you administer the poison?'

'In the sherry. She drinks a glass before dinner.'

'How will you get it into the glass?'

'Yes, that's a problem,' admitted the Duchess. 'Can't poison a whole bottle – might upset a few other people as well, and that'd be wrong. It'd be a damn sight easier if Hubert would co-operate, but he's hopeless, he won't agree to anything.'

'Oh, I know,' said Sir John with feeling. 'Angela is just the same. No team spirit.' He thought for a moment, and the air quivered slightly. 'I suggest you do this: when she gets her glass of sherry, knock it over accidentally, apologize profusely, and fetch her another into which you slip the poison.'

'Oh yes, I like that.'

'Just one word of advice, though, if I may. Do the thing discreetly. Don't just bring out a packet of weedkiller and pour the stuff in before the eyes of all.'

'Lord, no, I'll be careful. This is damn sportin' of you, Sir John.'

'Not at all,' replied Sir John, but this remark in fact sobered him. He was reminded that he did, after all, want Angela alive. In the fascination of planning this had slipped his memory.

'Tell me your own plans,' said the Duchess sympathetically.

'Yes,' said Sir John, cheering up. 'Implosion.'

'Oh no, friend, I can't agree with that,' said the Duchess, frowning. 'Damage to property. That's not right.'

'Not *ex*plosion, *im*plosion,' said Sir John. 'Exactly the opposite. I have a profound knowledge of science. I have a means of making him disappear into himself so that he will vanish leaving no trace.'

'What's Angela say to that?'

'She argued about prefixes for a while, but she's in favour, more or less, provided that she takes no part in it. It's a matter of making Hubert remain in his room, and finding some external means of wiring it up.'

'The wirin' bit is up to you,' said the Duchess, 'but I can make him stay in his room. I just have to tell him to make Angela go on ahead – he pretends he's searchin' for an adverbial artichoke, or somethin' – and wait for me to drop in on him.'

'That would be most generous of you!'

'One good turn deserves another.'

'I have to fix up the external device first,' said Sir John, 'but you must feel free to go ahead as soon as you like.'

'Will that be all right?'

'Certainly. No hard feelings. By the way, who was the young man who you say helped you to get the weed-killer?'

'Oh, you know, the very well-dressed one. He's in the police.'

'The *police*!'

'Yes. Nice to know they recruit a good class of person.'

'But, Duchess, really . . . !'

'Oh, don't worry. Nice lad.'

Mrs Hailstone was thinking about Mr Glossop. He had been naturally alarmed at meeting a woman with a gun, but it was still obvious to her that he was more afraid of imaginary women than real ones. Indeed, if the right woman could win his trust, he might be cured, and stop knocking valuable things over. She herself was really quite fond of him, for all his absurdity, or even because of it; it aroused her protective instinct. She studied herself in a hand mirror. She was in her mid-forties, slim, attractive, and quite young-looking, until, that is, she was measured against someone really young.

Like Harriet Gardiner.

M'm.

Mr Glossop had a way of looking at Harriet Gardiner. He never spoke to her, but he looked as if he wanted to.

He's nearly three times her age, thought Mrs Hailstone crossly.

But even that fact wasn't wholly reassuring. However, being a sensible person, she dismissed this train of thought completely.

But thinking of Harriet reminded her of Mr Norval. That young man was also given to looking at her. 'Sheep's eyes' was the expression, but in Mrs Hailstone's opinion a bad one, for sheep had yellow eyes with vertical slits and looked half-witted. 'Doe eyes' would be better. Eyes, anyway.

This did not surprise her – let's face it, the girl was stunning – but Mr Norval's general behaviour did. There was such a change in him. On the phone, the smooth salesman; at the reception desk, still smooth; but here in the hotel, increasingly unsure, puzzled, downcast. She actually liked him better like this, but he was staying at the hotel free, he was being paid to do so, and where was he getting? He did little else (when not eyeing Harriet) than stare at ceilings.

'Mr Norval – ' she began, having called him into her office.

'What you are about to say is quite sound,' he replied. 'I agree with it entirely.'

'Good,' she said, 'but I should be even more pleased if you would tell me what is going to *happen*.'

'I would, if it were tomorrow's share prices or the result of next year's Boat Race,' said Mr Norval, 'but what you want to know is unknowable.'

'Mr Norval, you did once reluctantly suggest murder – '

'Oh, that,' he said off-handedly, 'that's a charade. There's something else.'

'Oh yes? Something really serious? Mr Norval, will you please tell me just who is going to be murdered and when?'

'I didn't say anyone was. If you remember, I only said it was in the air.'

'You are quite the most annoying person I have ever met.'

'I know,' said Mr Norval humbly, 'I annoy myself intensely.'

Mrs Hailstone laughed helplessly, for she found it impossible to be cross with him for long. 'If everyone at Paranoics Anonymous is like you,' she said, 'I suspect they spread paranoia rather than cure it.'

'This is a very unusual case.'

'What *is* the case?'

'I don't know.'

'And what you don't know,' said Mrs Hailstone with exasperation, 'isn't knowledge. You really are infuriating.'

'You want me to pack this job in,' he suggested sadly.

Mrs Hailstone looked at him speculatively. He was maddening, but she felt, heaven help her, that in some incredible way he held the key to the Ariel's problems, if only someone could help him to find it. PC Mogpuss, her other researcher, was no doubt good at recording facts, but facts didn't seem available or even relevant in this case.

'No,' she said. 'Carry on for the time being.'

'Thank you,' said Mr Norval gratefully.

Mrs Hailstone saw him out. 'You'll probably find her working on the floor below this one,' she said.

This was a remark that he had *not* foretold. He blushed crimson, stammered something, and hastily took his leave.

Mrs Hailstone looked down from the banister rail to the strip of landing below. Sure enough, Harriet appeared, walking briskly, and Mr Norval, just as brisk, appeared from the opposite direction. Without slackening their pace, they for a fleeting instant held hands. Mrs Hailstone sighed gently and went back to her room.

Sir John Marvell, alias Mr Smith, went into the empty ground floor sitting-room, thinking hard. To fix up his Hubert-imploding apparatus was urgent. If the Duchess beat him to it with her attractively simple plan, he would be minus Angela and ten thousand pounds. Worse still, he would have lost, and he hated losing.

The Ariel, before becoming a hotel, had once been a stately home, and some appurtenances of that past era still hung about it. For instance, on the wall opposite the windows there was a bell-rope. In the old days one tugged it, and a liveried flunkey would appear. It was no longer in use, of course. But when Sir John spotted it his eyes lit up. He pointed to it with a shaking hand.

'A bell-rope!' he shouted exultantly. At that moment Hubert and Angela Toothpeace came in.

'What an extraordinary fellow,' remarked Hubert.

'Does every common object arouse him to a state of elementary excitement?' But Sir John did not hear this; he had hurried from the room to ascertain the exact alignment of that bell-rope with Hubert's room.

This, as he had guessed, was exactly above the sitting-room, but it was on the second floor. That meant that there was a room between it and the sitting-room. He would have to work on that room, both floor and ceiling, to connect to Hubert's. He could not afford to wait. But it was quite early in the morning, the occupants of that middle room would doubtless still be in it, and however unostentatiously he raised the floorboards and cut a hole in the ceiling, they would in all probability notice him.

He went to the first floor and studied the situation. He could hardly believe his luck. The room below Hubert's, and above the sitting-room, was not a bedroom but a store-room!

He fetched tools and apparatus and set to work on the store-room floor. He still had to work very discreetly, for the sitting-room below now contained several couples, and he had to cut through the highly ornamental ceiling of the stately home, with its massive coving and raised flight of cherubs chasing one another around blowing trumpets. But the occupants of the sitting-room, unlike Mr Norval, had no interest in ceilings, and so silently did Sir John work that he managed to remove a large square slab, wire up the bell-rope, and neatly replace the slab, without anyone's noticing. He was a superb workman, and if he had not spent his time winning the Nobel prize, swimming the Channel, etc., he could have been a master carpenter. Humming contentedly, he set to work on the store-room ceiling.

It happened that Harriet was tidying up the Tooth-peaces' room, while thinking unashamedly, or perhaps just a little ashamedly on Mavis's account, of Mr Norval. To her astonishment, the point of a saw came through the carpet and began to describe a circle. She watched, transfixed, as the circle was completed and pushed clear, like a manhole cover. She had a glimpse of Mr Smith just below the hole. He gripped the edge, preparatory to heaving himself into the room. He was between her and the door! She slipped into the bathroom, and found that she could watch him in the mirror above the washbasin. No longer flamboyant, a craftsman absorbed in his craft, he cut away a strip of wallpaper, ran a cable under it, patched it up perfectly, lowered his gear through the hole in the floor and himself after it, and pulled the 'manhole cover' after him with such exquisite precision that not a trace of the operation remained.

'Golly,' said Harriet, and came tremulously out of the bathroom.

She sat on the edge of one of the beds, shaken but calm.

It was clear that Mr Smith was up to no good!

Neither was Miss Hoskyn, for that matter. Harriet had never believed that she wanted weedkiller for a window-box.

Mr Smith and Miss Hoskyn were often seen together. Mavis must be right. Plotting!

And Mr Smith and Mrs Toothpeace, and Miss Hoskyn and Doctor Toothpeace, were also seen together, although not so frequently.

Suppose Miss Hoskyn was planning the murder of Mrs Toothpeace, and Mr Smith the murder of her husband!

Wait a minute, though. There was a flaw in this diagnosis. Mr Smith and Miss Hoskyn could hardly be *collaborating*, could they?

Curiouser and curiouser.

'I must tell Mavis,' she said.

Mavis was at the reception desk. Harriet slipped into the tiny office.

'Mavis, I must tell you – '

'I'm busy just now,' said Mavis, drawing down the corners of her mouth.

'You're not, you're reading the paper. Mavis, Mr Smith – '

'I don't want to hear.'

'Oh Mavis, do listen. All your theories are working out. Mr Smith – '

'I'm not interested.'

'Yes you are, of course you are. What's the matter with you?'

'I should go and ask *Norman*,' said Mavis bitterly.

Harriet was silenced. 'Oh dear,' she thought.

Mr Smith, alias Sir John Marvell, was on tenterhooks. His implosion device was in place; it needed only a tug on the bell-rope to implode Hubert Toothpeace into oblivion, but there was one snag: Hubert Toothpeace was never in his room alone. Perhaps the Duchess was, after all, reluctant to lure him there. Six o'clock p.m. came, and Hubert, still tiresomely in the company of his wife, went into the bar and ordered two sherries, which he carried to a table.

Miss Hoskyn rose and walked past them. It is pointless to describe her dress, as it was nondescript (she was happier in jodhpurs), but the skirt was full, and with a half-swing she contrived quite neatly to knock Angela's glass over without splashing Angela at all. Harriet hurried over to clean up the mess, and Sir John watched on edge as Miss Hoskyn apologized abjectly in a mouse-like voice and then, with all attention diverted from her, calmly filled a glass of sherry at the counter and tipped a white substance into it.

She took the glass to Angela's table, apologized again, and took her seat. Sir John's nerve gave. As Angela raised the glass to her lips, he started from his seat, pointed dramatically, and cried aloud, 'The sherry! The sherry!'

Hubert Toothpeace said coldly, 'Do you always shout with excitement at the immediately obvious?' and Angela took a sip.

And spat it out with unutterable disgust.

'It's full of *salt*!'

Hubert took the glass and tasted it judicially.

'*Full* is a slight exaggeration, but there is certainly a saline element.'

'It's *filthy*!' shrieked Angela, spluttering, grimacing, and rolling her tongue round her face like a cat. Miss Hoskyn came up, or perhaps one should say the Duchess of Sligo did. She was furious at the failure of her scheme, and her eyes were blazing. But before she could speak, PC Mogpuss, in a contemporary single-breasted camel colour doeskin blazer and glencheck trousers with front pleats and turn-ups, hurried over to her.

'Madam, you are not to blame yourself for this. I strongly suspect a male person in this room.' He looked sternly at Sir John, who was excusably looking bland with relief. 'My suspicions were aroused when he shouted in that incriminating way!'

Whereupon the Duchess became Miss Hoskyn again, murmured something, and left the room, as did Angela, spluttering; as did Hubert, following; as did Sir John, smirking. Harriet looked round the half-emptied room, where several couples were steadfastly taking no notice. If only she could talk to Mavis about this.

'Salt!' said the Duchess with fury. 'The packet's clearly marked weedkiller, dammit. What's that old fool of a gardener playin' at?'

'Show me the packet,' said Sir John soothingly. He was sincerely sorry for the Duchess in her disappointment. Indeed, his sympathy fairly balanced his relief that Angela had escaped death. 'Ah yes,' he said, when the Duchess fetched it from her bedside cabinet, 'this is three years out of date. The gardener used the contents long ago, and keeps the packet to store salt.'

'What the hell does the old fool do that for?'

'Well, salt is a weedkiller. One teaspoonful will kill a dandelion.'

'He should have told me. Servants today have no sense of duty.'

'What did Hubert have to say?'

'Not much sympathy there. He seemed more sorry for his *wife*, dammit. About my plan, he just said he couldn't tolerate inexactitude. As if it were my fault.'

'The sooner he's imploded the better,' said Sir John, indignant at this injustice to his friend.

'Ah yes,' said the Duchess. 'Up to me to make him keep to his room, what?'

'You're still willing?' said Sir John, deeply moved.

'A bargain's a bargain,' said the Duchess. 'They'll be comin' down to dinner in about an hour's time. Stand by, Sir John. I'll fix it.'

Greater love had no woman than that she would lay down her lover's life for a friend, misquoted Sir John to himself with emotion. He spent the time before dinner pacing his room and ejaculating 'ha!' in a muted voice. For all his masterful ways he was more nervous than the Duchess, and when she looked round the door of the ground floor sitting-room and gave him a wink, he wondered at her composure, and also her self-sacrifice, which he considered equal to that of the hero of *A Tale of Two Cities*. Not knowing much about human nature, having been too busy winning the Heavyweight Championship, etc., he did not know that the Duchess in a perverse way was enjoying herself.

He made as if to leave the room and gave the bell-rope an unobtrusive tug as he passed. As he entered the dining-room a squelching noise sounded from above, as if a wet plunger had been pulled sharply away from a tiled floor. He passed Angela at her table, formally

48

acknowledged her, and murmured in her ear, 'You left him in your room?'

She nodded. 'He was searching for a cognative object.'

'He is searching no longer. He is imploded.'

Angela rose quietly and went up to her room. If she found nothing there, signifying that her husband had utterly disintegrated, she would, in spite of herself, be as distressed as if her handbag were missing. She entered the room. There was not nothing there. There was Hubert, covered from head to foot in a white substance. It much impeded his progress. He could only stand, his legs apart and his arms held away from his body, his mouth opening and shutting like an air-bubble in cement, but he was clearly alive. Angela cried out in vexation:

'You haven't been crawling up chimneys again?'

Hubert replied with difficulty but also with dignity: '(a) there is no chimney in this room; (b) soot is not white.'

Angela answered: '(a) there are chimneys elsewhere in this erstwhile stately home and (b) there may be white soot of a rare kind. For instance, there is a kind of white chocolate.'

She looked about her. There was no trace of the white substance on the carpet or the beds, but when she looked at the ceiling she saw what it was, for all the plaster had been sucked away, exposing bare plaster boards. By a miracle of implosion the entire quantity had settled on Hubert.

She was thankful for this small piece of fortune, for she was a tidy person, but shocked at the damage to the ceiling. As she stood there Sir John Marvell appeared in the doorway. He was, as we are discovering, a much more sensitive man than at first appeared. He was sorry to see her distressed. He exclaimed involuntarily, 'Dear Heart – '

'This, sir,' said Hubert, 'is my wife, not a brand of dog food!'

Angela bustled Sir John into the corridor.

'I must tell you that I am not impressed with your mastery of science. If your financial skills are not better, you could hardly govern a piggy-bank.'

'Angela – '

'Oh, go and climb Mount Everest or something!'

Hubert, plodding stiffly, now joined them in the corridor.

Sir John Marvell may have been a potential murderer, but he was a gentleman.

'You have been rather put about, Doctor Toothpeace,' he said. 'I commiserate with you for any inconvenience you have been caused.'

Hubert, unaware of Mr Smith's part in the affair, felt that he deserved a courteous response. 'I appreciate your sentiments, sir,' he said civilly, 'even though your bad style disgusts me.'

Mr Smith walked moodily out of the hotel grounds the next morning, and PC Mogpuss, in a subtly trimmed plain navy-blue cardigan, green sportsman cord trousers and paisley shirt, strolled casually in his wake. He went into the wood, and the policeman ensconced himself in a thicket and took notes. A minute later Miss Hoskyn turned up, her stride lengthening as she drew away from the hotel, and went into the wood after him. Unfortunately, the thicket in which the policeman had ensconced himself was too far away for him to hear their conversation, and the foliage was too thick for him to see them any more, but he took notes anyway, from force of habit.

'Angela is totally unreasonable,' growled Sir John, seated on the familiar log. 'She simply won't acknowledge the brilliance of what I did. Technically it was masterly. The mere fact that it failed in its object is negligible.'

'Hubert's just as bad. He won't see that the fault lies with that old fool of a gardener, not me.'

'How is he, by the way?'

'Oh, most of it's scraped off. He's just a rather unbecomin' shade of grey all over. But still tiresome. They're an annoyin' pair. They don't appreciate what we're doin' for them.'

'No, they don't. I wonder whether they're worth the trouble.'

'Hey, wait a minute,' exclaimed the Duchess. 'You're not thinkin' of packin' it in, are you?'

'It had crossed my mind,' muttered Sir John.

'Now, friend, this will never do. We've put our hands to the plough, what?'

'You're still game?' demanded Sir John with admiration.

'Never say die, what?'

'Duchess, you're a wonderful woman. I'm ashamed of my cowardly thoughts. I'll go on.'

'That's the spirit!' cried the Duchess, and clumped him so heartily that he was reminded of the seventh round of his Heavyweight Championship bout, when his opponent put him on the canvas for a short count.

6

As we have seen, Harriet had progressed from 'sir' to
'Norman' in a few days, and now talked to him freely. He
was as pleased as she was; a weight seemed to have been
lifted from him. 'I was just a negative looking for a
positive,' he told her. Harriet thought this very romantic,
as well as being pleasingly different from young men's
conventional endearments.

'But you're not a detective after all,' she said regretfully, for this would be another disappointment to the
already disgruntled Mavis.

'No, on official forms I put myself down as a consul-
tant.'

'And you're not mad,' said Harriet. Norman looked
uncertain. 'Oh well,' said Harriet, 'just a *bit* mad,
perhaps.' Recalling St Phocas and the marble woman,
she reconsidered. 'That was mad all right,' she said.
'What were you talking about?'

'I just don't know,' said Norman. 'Usually I know
exactly, including things that are going to happen, like
the poems of Ted Hughes. It helps to sort out what's real
from what's imagined. Our work usually means helping
real people to get rid of imaginary fears. But here, it's the
people themselves who seem to me imaginary, and
somehow trying to be real.'

'What about Mr Glossop? His fears are imaginary,
aren't they?'

'Yes, but he puzzles me. I'm sure that putting them right is a very little thing, like putting a fuse in a plug, but I can't see what it is.'

Harriet told him about Dominic Deverell, Hannibal Harbinger, and all the other aliases with which Mr Glossop covered sheets of paper. 'He doesn't seem to like his own name,' she remarked. 'He could change it by deed-poll, I suppose.'

'That wouldn't help,' said Norman. 'He'd still be Glossop under the skin. But this is valuable evidence.'

'Is it?' said Harriet, gratified. 'Evidence of what?'

'I don't know.'

'I *do* know why Mrs Hailstone wants to kill you sometimes,' said Harriet. 'You talk in riddles. What about Mr Smith and Miss Hoskyn? I'm sure they're up to no good.'

'Ah, that's a charade.'

'But you told Mrs Hailstone there was murder in the air. Is it them?' He nodded. 'But you say that's just make-believe?' He nodded again. 'Well, I suppose that's all right, then,' said Harriet.

'Not altogether,' said Norman. 'People can get hurt playing games.'

'Oh dear, dear,' said Harriet. 'Riddles again. I must go, anyway.' At the door she turned back. 'Hang on,' she said. 'You *are* a detective after all. You're detecting, aren't you? You're not a professional, but neither are the ones that Mavis likes – they're priests or dukes or – or old maids and so on. Amateurs. You're a detective and, not to stretch it too much, a mad one too.'

'Nice to know,' said Norman.

'Do something for me, Norman. Go and tell Mavis that you are a detective and that you need a girl assistant.'

'I've got one already, it seems to me.'

'Make her your official one. She'll be thrilled to bits.'

'I can't just walk up to her and say – '

'Listen carefully,' said Harriet.

*

The relationship of Harriet and Norman expressed itself as yet only in fleeting touches of fingertips, but it was exquisite, this very marginal love play, and already she felt new power in her veins. It was as if his rare gift had somehow communicated itself. Not that she could foretell the future, but her intuition was heightened. And she knew that what he had said about Mr Glossop – that some tiny adjustment would put him right – also applied, mysteriously, to Norman himself. For he did need adjusting; although he was happy to have found his 'positive', he was not completely happy, and it had something to do with his name. Norman Norval. But here Harriet's intuition gave out, and she felt some of his own frustration, seeing in a glass darkly, unable to get what she saw into focus. (Phocas?) She shook her head angrily, but did not clear it.

Mr Glossop continued to give her strange looks. She did not mind. His were not the looks that middle-aged men so often gave girls. But they were certainly strange. He seemed to be looking for help, somehow, but she had no idea what help she could give him, and neither, she was sure, had he.

One day he actually spoke to her.

'Everything all right, Harriet?'

'Yes thank you, sir.'

'Good, good. We're very pleased with your work. The guests like you too.'

'Thank you, sir.'

'They never complain about the service in any way, do they? We aim at perfection.'

There was one very small thing. There had been a minor grumble at the breakfast table. The Ariel served those who wanted it with an 'innkeeper's breakfast'. It consisted of a chop, several rashers of bacon, two fried eggs, mushrooms, fried potatoes, fried tomatoes and fried bread. Harriet, who ate one piece of toast for breakfast, recoiled at the sight of it. But one guest, a pudding of a man with a white slab of a face, and heading inevitably towards a heart attack, had asked for sausages as well.

'It's hardly worth mentioning, sir,' Harriet told Mr Glossop, 'but – '

But when she uttered the word 'sausages', Mr Glossop's veins stood out.

'Don't mention that word!'

'All right, sir.'

'Never!'

'No, all right, sir.'

He looked at her face, which, happening to be caught in a certain light, was like an angel's, and was overcome with contrition.

'I'm sorry, I shouldn't have shouted at you. I'm sorry, it's not your fault. You're not upset, are you?'

'It's all right, sir.'

'He has a phobia,' she said to herself.

Mavis pushed Harriet's door open and came in with two mugs of cocoa and a packet of Cadbury's Roses. Harriet sat up in bed, glowing.

'Oh, Mavis! For me?'

'I'm sorry I was rotten,' said Mavis. 'You were right, Harriet, I've got a nasty, suspicious nature. I had no reason to be, of you of all people, and I'm ashamed of myself.'

'So what's happened to make you change your mind?' said Harriet, smiling.

'Harriet, I hardly like to tell you – '

'Go on, I won't make a scene.'

'It's Norman, Harriet. We had such a long talk. He *is* a detective.'

'Well, you spotted that right away.'

'Well, I did, didn't I?' said Mavis, beaming. 'Harriet, he's told me about some right goings on at this hotel! That Hoskyn has got hold of some weedkiller – '

'No!'

'She has. And wait till you hear this. Smith cut a hole in the floor of Toothpeace's room and fixed up some kind of bomb in it, and the ceiling fell in!'

'I say! Norman told you a thing or two, didn't he?'

'Well, this is it. He says I'm very observant.'

'So you are.'

' – and just the kind of person he could use. Look, Harriet, don't take this wrong, but he's asked me to be his assistant!'

'Great! You're the very one for the job!'

'Oh, Harriet. Oh, I don't know what to say. Oh it's smashing of you to take it so well, Harriet – '

'Have a chocolate.'

'No, no, they're for you. Oh, I am chuffed, Harriet. This is what I've always wanted.'

'You deserve it.' Harriet smiled at her friend, well pleased with the success of her scheme. She noticed that Mavis was still dressed. 'Not going to bed yet?' she said.

'No, I'm meeting Norman in the lounge.'

'Oh? So late?'

'Well, I'm helping him with his inquiries.'

'Oh. Good.'

'So long as I keep my mind on the subject,' said Mavis, grinning. 'I mean, he's dishy, isn't he? Well, mustn't keep him waiting. Goodnight, sweetie. Sleep well.' And she parted from Harriet with great affection.

Harriet lay in bed thinking it over. That *had* worked out well.

'Greater love hath no girl,' she said to herself ruefully.

PC Mogpuss, wearing an American-Indian fringed poncho in white, caught in with a beaded belt, spoke earnestly into the phone.

'I am convinced that this man Smith has some evil hold over Miss Hoskyn, Sergeant. This morning he lured her into a wood.'

'It's not for the Force to judge people's morals – '

'I think it's a matter of crime, not morals. A strange thing happened last night . . .' And he told the sergeant about Angela and the sherry, and of Smith's choking cry just as she had been about to drink it. 'His face,' he said, 'was suffused with passion.

'It is a brutal face at the best of times,' he went on. 'As I have informed you, Miss Hoskyn is evidently a member of the upper classes, and it may be that the man Smith, whose bestial features obviously lack gentility, was a former groom or chauffeur of hers, and is in possession of some incriminating secret, some letters, perhaps, which the poor woman wrote in the trusting innocence of her youth – '

'Hold on,' said the sergeant, 'we're not living in Edwardian times. Who cares about letters nowadays?'

'The tabloid press might.'

'All right, but where is this leading to?'

'My belief is that the scoundrel Smith is contriving to murder Mrs Angela Toothpeace, who very likely knows some dark secret of his, and is using Miss Hoskyn to further his nefarious ends.'

'You can't arrest someone on just a belief, Officer. Has anything actually happened?'

'Well, no. The ceiling of the Toothpeaces' room fell in last night, and Mrs Toothpeace's husband was covered in plaster, but the man Smith couldn't possibly have had anything to do with that.'

Mr Glossop was distressed to hear about the collapse of the Toothpeaces' ceiling, which he naturally attributed to a structural defect, and deputed Mrs Hailstone to offer them another room.

But Angela wouldn't hear of it. She was a highly conscientious woman, so much so that she was even reluctant to participate in her husband's murder, and she knew that the ceiling disaster was no fault of the Ariel Hotel's.

'We seldom look at the ceiling,' she assured Mrs Hailstone, 'and parts of the room are excellent. Please think no more about it.'

'What I can't understand,' said Mrs Hailstone, 'is how all the plaster fell on Doctor Toothpeace, and none on the floor.'

Angela had to improvise an explanation quickly.

'My husband noticed the plaster beginning to fall, and before it could reach the ground he managed to catch the whole lot on his person by springing about the room.'

'No I didn't,' interrupted Hubert.

'You did, my dear,' said Angela quickly and emphatically. 'You showed remarkable presence of mind and quite extraordinary agility.'

'Oh, did I?' said Hubert, gratified. The plaster had, in fact, fallen on him like an avalanche.

'I assure you you did.'

'Then my recollection must be erroneous,' said Hubert. 'I wonder, however, if one might say *alacrity* rather than *agility*?'

'Yes, indeed one might,' conceded Angela. They had not been in such agreement for months.

Angela was frankly sorry for Hubert, who had been made both ridiculous and uncomfortable, and also sorry for herself, for it is degrading to have a ridiculous husband. Yet, with the perversity of human nature, she was annoyed with herself for feeling sorry, because it weakened her resolve to let Hubert be murdered, and even more annoyed with Sir John for causing her to feel sorry.

Sir John defended his device, but with a little less of his usual overweening confidence.

'In principle it worked perfectly, but it was employed in too large a space,' he said. 'Ideally, Hubert should be imploded in a confined space, like for instance a coffin.'

'I'm sure one could acquire a coffin,' replied Angela. 'The problem would be inducing Hubert to get into it. "Look, dear, I've purchased this fine old antique coffin in the village. What fun if you lay in it while I nailed down the lid." His suspicions might well be aroused.'

'I shall bend all my prodigious faculties to the solution of this,' said Sir John, smarting a little, for there was no mistaking the sarcasm in her words.

His confidence was, in truth, undermined. At first, Angela had seemed such an easy conquest – he the man of power, she the submissive female – but he had discovered that she had a power all her own. She also had an inflexible will, although bodily she was, as it were, flexible – to such an extent that her skeleton seemed hardly capable of holding her upright. And she had a woman's terrible gift for unmanning a man. Consequently, from being her surrogate lord and master, Sir John was turning into something like a slave, anxious to please.

His comfort in this troubled period was his friend the Duchess, a sympathetic and encouraging confidante. As for her, her next plan to kill Angela was even more straightforward than the first. She aimed to drop a huge stone pot on her from a third-floor balcony. The only problem was how to make Angela stand exactly underneath it and keep still.

'The solution,' said Sir John, when she confided in him, 'will be to have her photograph taken in that spot. She would have to stand still for minutes on end.'

'But while I'm up there poisin' the bally pot,' said the Duchess, 'who's goin' to take the photo? You couldn't ask your average photographer to position her that accurately, dammit.'

After a long pause, during which he wrestled with his natural reluctance, Sir John answered, 'I will. I am a master of disguises, and she will have no idea who the photographer is. Pretending to seek the perfect pose, I will position her unerringly and signal to you when to act.'

'That's dashed sportin' of you, Sir John. Now how are your own plans progressin'?'

They were conferring this time in Sir John's own room. He produced a big diagram and spread it out on the floor.

'I have ascertained that Hubert Toothpeace adjusts his tie, brushes his hair, etc., in front of the long mirror in the hotel wardrobe,' he stated. 'Once I have made sure that he is standing in the right spot, the rest will be easy. I have only to tug the bell-rope as before, and his implosion will be assured.'

'That's where I come in again,' said the Duchess, with less reluctance than Sir John had shown. 'I'll buy Hubert a fancy tie, and get him to put it on in front of the mirror. How shall I signal to you when he's in place? Ah, I know. I'll step into the corridor and fire my gun. Just listen for the bang, and then don't hang about, pull that bell-rope.'

'Won't you attract people's attention?'

'Don't worry about them. The people here pretend not to notice things. You saw how they behaved over that sherry business. Don't give it another thought. This diagram looks frightfully clever.'

'No, once I have fixed it all up, it will have a beautiful simplicity. See here. When I pull the bell-rope, it will release the spring-catch, James, behind the wardrobe door, which I have called Elspeth. This will cause the door, Elspeth, to slam violently to, pitching Hubert Toothpeace into the wardrobe itself, which on this plan I have indicated as Herbert Ferguson. Fractionally later, the semi-circular steel bands, Sappho and Rhinox, snap round him and pinion his arms. Their action automatically indents the button, Ferdie, causing the floor of the wardrobe, Myrtle, to rise, and the roof, Alexis, to descend. (I have indicated their motion by the dotted line, Habbakuk.) As his head touches Alexis – a matter of half a second – implosion will take place, the wardrobe door, Elspeth, will fly open, and complete normality will be resumed, except that Hubert Toothpeace will have vanished.'

'Great,' said the Duchess, rather dazedly.

'The idea of using names instead of the usual letters on this diagram – you like that?'

'Oh, sure.'

'I felt that it lent the diagram a certain friendly warmth?'

'I don't doubt it, old pal. What does Angela think?'

'She hasn't seen it yet.'

'Bet she finds fault with it.'

But this was a bet he didn't care to take.

7

Although Sir John Marvell made light of his latest invention, it was clearly a masterpiece of engineering and a tribute to his genius. The present writer, who finds even the mechanism of a bicycle beyond his grasp, is fairly stunned with wonder at it. Sir John had one weakness, though; so absorbed was he with fitting it up that he was careless about being overlooked. It so happened that as he pushed his way for a second time through the Toothpeaces' floor, Harriet was again in their room, tidying it up.

Once again, she slipped into the bathroom to watch his actions. Head and shoulders out of the hole, he made some adjustments to something below, and then, heaving himself into the room, he began working on the wardrobe. This was out of range of the bathroom mirror, but Harriet could tell from his movements that a contraption of considerable complexity was being rigged up.

He stood back, contemplated his handiwork, said 'Ha!' with quiet satisfaction, and made his exit through the hole again, leaving no trace.

Harriet struggled with her conscience. She really ought to report Mr Smith's raids on the Toothpeaces' room.

But hadn't Norman dismissed his antics as 'a charade'? A charade was a game. Perhaps Mr Smith was doing all this just for a lark, as one might make an apple-pie bed.

He was sometimes seen in Angela's company, and perhaps he and the Toothpeaces were old friends, merrily given to playing pranks on one another.

She knew that all this was most specious, but she clung to it just the same. The truth was that she was extremely reluctant to report to anyone, either PC Mogpuss or Norman and his perky assistant or even Mrs Hailstone. If she did she would simply be the room-maid-witness, like the maid in Mavis's favourite kind of story, whose function was solely to find the body and scream, and who was briefly questioned by the smart alec sleuth (*and* his perky assistant!) and then disappeared from the story altogether while the clever ones did their clever stuff. Well, to hell with that.

She was at war with herself. Urging Norman to make 'an assistant' of Mavis had succeeded all too well. She was sincerely fond of Mavis. The trouble was that Norman threatened to become equally so. And Mavis could be quite a danger. Harriet knew herself to be beautiful, but her beauty was of the kind that often puts young men off; they feel that they can't cope with such quality and shy away. But Mavis was a kitten ideal for a frolic. Harriet was Norman's equal, and a slightly superior equal at that. Mavis would be his adoring underling, and a tonic to his self-esteem. The more she thought about it, the more Harriet saw her friendly move as a self-sacrifice.

She had for some time cherished a day-dream in which she and Norman were married and enjoyed a life of bliss by the judicious manipulation of his gift. They would never want for money, because he would only have to back a horse or sell some shares at the right time. (Yes, he was much opposed to backing predicted horses, etc., and so was she, in principle, but just now and *then*, when it was absolutely *necessary* . . .) They would not go in for excess, you understand. Not luxury for its own sake. Not untold wealth. Just a lovely house, a brand new car, posh furniture, glamorous holidays . . .

They would never quarrel, because he would see the quarrel coming and adroitly avoid it . . .

But now, as she miserably drank a cup of coffee in the staff pantry, by herself, because Mavis was probably helping Norman with his enquiries, she saw this day-dream fade, and another replaced it with Mavis taking over from herself.

She went glumly back to work. Resentment of Norman set in. If he really could foretell the future, why hadn't he foretold Mavis's intrusion into her, Harriet's, happiness, and prevented it?

Perhaps he didn't want to prevent it!

The inconstancy of men!

She decided that she hated him. Definitely. Hated him.

She was very unhappy. But no one could say that Harriet was lacking in spirit. If you can't join 'em, beat 'em, she said to herself bravely. Had Mavis read any stories where rival detectives competed to solve a mystery? Well, now she was going to *be in one*. Some strange things were going on in the Ariel Hotel, and she, Harriet, would sort them out single-handed, and leave the mad detective and his winsome assistant stranded in her wake.

Her resolve was nearly undone in the very next minute. As she stepped briskly along the first floor corridor Norman happened to come face-to-face with her. He reached out to touch her hand as they sailed past each other. But she steeled herself, kept her arms at her sides, looked straight ahead, and hurried on. Norman halted, his arm still foolishly stuck out. He looked hurt and bewildered, but she didn't see him, and prided herself on handling that little incident nicely.

*

64

With all of an artist's anxious fondness for his creation, Sir John showed his diagram to Angela. But the brilliance of the device was lost on her, for she took the whole world of technology for granted.

'So Hubert is to look at himself in the wardrobe mirror. What then? Will he fall in love with himself and turn into a narcissus?'

With exemplary patience, Sir John explained everything again.

'You will see that I have used names on the diagram instead of letters,' he said hopefully.

'That I do not care for,' said Angela, 'because you have mixed up English, Greek and Biblical ones, which I think inconsistent.'

This hurt him, because he had used the names especially to please her; but it was a pathetic effort, miles wide of its mark. She did not wish to be pleased. She craved to be mastered; but as soon as that process began, she did her best to thwart it, and so baffled her own desires.

They parted coolly. Sir John smouldered with a sense of injustice and the beginnings of a terrible self-doubt.

The Duchess was sympathetic. 'She deserves to have a huge stone pot dropped on her as soon as poss.,' she said.

How much, in his heart, did he agree! His feelings confused and dismayed him.

The Duchess had discussed her own plan with Hubert. The brutality of it did not shock him, because, locked in a gaol of words, he could not take the physical world seriously. 'So the huge stone pot falls on Angela from a height,' he observed, 'and then, SPLAT!' And having used this dreadful expression from the comics, he blushed and giggled gleefully. Then he added anxiously, 'You don't think ZONK! WHAM! or POW! perhaps? – No; SPLAT is clearly the correct word. It is a derivative of *splatter* . . .'

And then, just for the moment, he peeped out of his gaol of words and realized the implications of what he had just said. But only for the moment. He had found the *mot juste*, and that was all that mattered.

He returned to his own room. He had had several baths by now, and had sent his suit to the cleaners, and was his dapper self again. Angela was still quite sympathetic. She even put his tie straight in a wifely manner, and looked him up and down.

'Perfectly presentable,' she said. 'Not a trace remains.'

'Perhaps one should say *vestige*?' said Hubert.

'One might, equally well,' said Angela kindly.

He began to admire himself in the wardrobe mirror, but his wife suddenly protested. 'Not the wardrobe, Hubert. There is a good mirror in the bathroom. Or one in front of the dressing table.'

'What's wrong with this one?' he asked, surprised.

'It – it isn't in a very good light.'

'It's in a perfect light. See for yourself.'

He led her to the wardrobe. Her image stared back at her accusingly. She agreed about the light, defeated. He was momentarily puzzled by the uneasy way she had stepped before the mirror. It was almost as if she had stepped on to a scaffold.

Mr Glossop had always banned sausages from the Ariel's menus. His chefs, who were French, thought this was just good taste, for they despised sausages as vulgar German things. But his aversion, as we know, went right back to the Infants' School, when he had been insultingly compared to one. Now fifty, he had forgotten the squeaky little girls, and so was unaware of the source of his fears. But since Harriet had innocently brought up the subject of sausages, he had become more fearful than ever, and took to slinking into Mrs Hailstone's office more often.

She thought it dreadful that a man of such great

achievements could have such a weakness, and she was growing more and more convinced that he needed the help of a good woman, a real one, to chase away those frightful females of the instincts that distressed him so much.

'Mr Glossop,' she ventured, as he peered fearfully out of her window, 'has it ever occurred to you that I am a woman?'

'No, Mrs Hailstone, you are a *femme supérieure*.'

'Thank you,' said Mrs Hailstone, colouring with pleasure.

'If more women were like you,' said Mr Glossop, 'the world would be a better place. I hardly like to say this – '

'Mr Glossop, please go on.'

'Don't take this as idle flattery, Mrs Hailstone – '

'I won't!'

'I think of you as a vortex of efficiency.'

'Oh.'

'Oh yes. So cool, so capable, so poised. The vulgar emotions seem to have no part in you. I look on you, Mrs Hailstone, as one might look on a beautifully balanced machine.'

'Well!' said Mrs Hailstone, when he had gone, 'it's nice to know I rate as high as a weighing-machine. I wonder if he feels the same about Harriet?' But it is a tribute to her good nature that she bore Harriet no rancour.

Oscar Wilde tells us that each man kills the thing he loves. Well, Sir John Marvell was certainly taking his part in the killing of Angela whole-heartedly, even with relish. It was beginning to look like more than mere good sportsmanship.

On the following day a photographer came into the Ariel. He had a big blond beard and a leonine mane of yellow hair. He spoke with a French accent. He had a way of making a circle with his forefinger and thumb and jerking it up to the level of his eyebrow. While in conversation with the receptionist he did this several times, describing the village of Mockery Hollow as but charming, the grounds outside as but exquisite, and the hotel itself as but magnificent.

Various guests drifted out of the hotel without attracting more than a glance from him; but soon Angela and Hubert Toothpeace came on their way to the village, arm in arm, and to outward appearances a contented married couple. The photographer sprang in front of Angela, made a circle out of his forefinger and thumb, kissed it, and flicked if aloft as if he were throwing a dart.

'But *yes*!' he cried ecstatically. 'Oh but *yes*!'

'No, sir,' replied Hubert – he was always polite to foreigners – '*yes* is a particle equivalent to an affirmative sentence, and can only be used in answer to a question. As for *but*,' but Angela, looking at the stranger with interest, said, 'Let us hear further, Hubert. I think we can take "but yes" merely as an expletive, prefacing a more expansive exposition,' and the photographer was allowed to deliver a series of 'but ravishings' and 'but perfections', while Angela contemplated him with increasing favour.

'He wants to take my photograph, Hubert,' she said. 'Free.'

'But naturally,' cried the photographer, 'to demand payment for the sheer delight of capturing perfection would be but sordid, but profane.'

It was a terrible piece of ham acting, but it worked. Indeed, when flattering people of either sex it is impossible to ham it up too much. The flatteree should be as thickly coated as Hubert was by the plaster.

The photographer was emphatic as to where the picture should be taken. It must be by the side of the stone lion on the left. In this way, female perfection would be shown against a perfect background. Dress? Ah, that was *sans importance*. But Angela didn't think so, and went off to change, returning after a long delay in a

68

high-waisted silver gown that reached to her feet and made her look a flexible Britannia and a fitting complement to the lion.

The Duchess, meanwhile, had taken up her position on the balcony directly above the stone lion. This is easier said than it was done. The hotel's balconies were all private to the rooms, and to get there she had to climb up to the roof, crawl over it, and shin down a drain-pipe. To allay any suspicions of the people in the room behind this balcony she had disguised herself (not very convincingly, truth to tell) as a window-cleaner, by tying up her hair in a duster and carrying a pail of water. Luckily she found that the curtains of the room in question were still drawn, and she was able to concentrate on her task.

Hubert now realized what this was all about, and it cannot be denied that he watched his wife being carefully positioned for her destruction with some misgivings. He might even have intervened, but he was fretting over the question as to whether 'But *yes!*' could properly be called an expletive, or whether *interjection* would be better. Angela posed gracefully by the lion, the photographer bent to his camera, and the Duchess, above, pushed the huge stone pot off its ledge.

But Fate intervened. As she did so, she disturbed a wasp that had been dozing by the pot on the ledge. Cross at being aroused, it zoomed down and buzzed into Angela's face. She naturally jumped aside, flapping at it, and the huge stone pot struck the spot where she had just been standing, bounced, and knocked the ear off the stone lion.

A number of passing guests had paused to watch Angela being photographed. 'That might have been a nasty accident,' they told one another, and went on to browse round the shops in the village. The Duchess shook her head over her truly rotten luck, shinned up the wall to the top floor and made her way down via the roof, while PC Mogpuss, wearing a tweed jacket with velvet collar, velvet trousers and a satin T-shirt, went hunting furiously for Mr Smith, strongly suspecting him of being responsible for the accident; but of course he never found him, and reluctantly decided that after all he couldn't possibly have had anything to do with it.

8

Harriet still shared mugs of cocoa with Mavis when they went to bed. She would only be putting herself in the wrong if she didn't, and besides, Mavis was still basically likeable, even though she was alienating the affections of the love of Harriet's life. For that, now that she couldn't have him, was what Harriet had decided Norman must be. Of course it was absurd. Even so quickly could one catch the plague? She didn't even *like* him much. She still thought he was weird. And irritating beyond belief. Yes, but she was mystically convinced that he could be cured of those qualities and emerge transformed and shining, and that she alone could find the cure. Alas, she would never be allowed to do so. He and she would join the tragic young lovers of legend. She wept, but only into her pillow when alone. For Mavis she kept a smiling face.

And for Norman a stony one. At first he had made half-moves to speak to her, but not for her life would she respond, and he was obliged to follow suit, so that now they passed each other in corridors like sleepwalkers with tunnel vision. Two minutes of explanation would have cleared everything up, but they were in love, and being as pig-headed as possible.

'So how's the detective work going?' she asked Mavis brightly.

'Well, not all that well, I don't think.'

'No?' said Harriet, not displeased.

'No, he doesn't take any notice of the things that I reckon matter. I know that private detectives are supposed to be all secretive and keep you guessing, so that they can spring the solution on you in the end, like when everyone's gathered in the library – '

'Mavis, what isn't he taking notice of?'

'Well, he's not trailing that Hoskyn any more. Or Smith. Well, they *are* the mystery of the Ariel Hotel, aren't they? I'm sure they've got it in for the Toothpeaces. You've heard how Mrs T. nearly got killed the other morning, haven't you? And how the ceiling fell in on old Dr Toothpeace? Well surely those things mean something? But when I mention them to Norman he just says, "Oh, that," and looks all indifferent. I don't know about mad detective. More like dozy detective I reckon. In a trance half the time. He doesn't seem very happy to me.'

'No?' said Harriet, with kindling hope.

'No, and when he goes into this trance he mumbles something about St Phocas. St Phocas is that statue in the little house in the grounds – '

'Yes, I know.'

'Well, whatever's a statue got to do with it?'

What indeed. But mention of St Phocas oddly consoled Harriet, reminding her of that early meeting.

'He talks sometimes,' said Mavis, 'as if he knew what was going to happen.'

So Norman hadn't told Mavis of his gift. Not on such intimate terms with her? Harriet's hope kindled a little more brightly.

'I asked him outright about it,' said Mavis. ' "You seem to know the future," I said. Oh he said, the future looks after itself. So what does matter, then, I said, the past? Not so much the past, he said, as our memory of the past. I suppose that means something, I said, quite sarcastically, but it's too clever for me.'

Nor could Harriet understand it, but it touched a chord

in her somewhere. She wondered now if she might even ask him to explain, using this as a means of breaking their silence. Instead of waiting for him to leave his room before she tidied it, she could come upon him by accident . . .

'You know what, Harriet?' said Mavis. 'I reckon he's in love.'

Harriet, blushing deeply, pulled her face back into the shadow cast by her bedside lamp, and said, 'Mavis, that's ridiculous!'

'Oh well, thanks, sweetie,' said Mavis. 'You reckon I'm so repulsive, then?'

'Oh! No, no, of course not!'

'He looks at me with this sort of lovesick look on his face,' said Mavis. 'Actually men do fancy me, Harriet, though I say it myself.'

'I'm sure they do, Mavis,' said Harriet with feeling.

'He's got me quite worried,' said Mavis. 'It's quite a responsibility, you know.'

'Oh, you'll handle it, I'm sure,' said Harriet brightly – well, indeed, hectically – while she felt her heart sinking like a plumb weight into bottomless depths. Lost, lost.

PC Mogpuss was window-shopping in the High Street of Mockery Hollow, where the clothes shops all but alternated with those that sold antiques. He had already acquired an extensive wardrobe, but he feared that it was a little conventional – i.e. a trouser still adorned each leg – and he was considering the possibilities of a kilt, complete with sporran and a skean-dhu down the stocking, with a protruding handle made of deer's antler. A complete outfit would be needed, including a tasteful tam o' shanter. But was it in order for one to become a kind of honorary Scotsman? He was a stickler for good form. He was debating the matter with himself when a voice said 'Hallo', and he turned to face Miss Hoskyn.

Or perhaps the Duchess of Sligo; or some of both. In

the dialogue that followed, her voice rose and fell as if a volume control inside her was being continually raised and lowered. She was, as we have seen, careless in sustaining her role as Miss Hoskyn; she was careless in every sort of dealing, as she had an inborn faith that she was above the law and that the rest of humanity was bound to accept her at face value, whatever face she chose to put on. To begin with, however, she was Miss Hoskyn.

'Excuse me,' she said timidly, 'I wonder if I might ask you for some advice?'

'Why, of course, madam. Certainly, madam. By all means, madam.' PC Mogpuss was delighted; not only was this lady a member of the upper classes, but he regarded her as his protégée.

'I couldn't help noticing,' said Miss Hoskyn, still timid, 'that you have excellent taste in dress.'

'O-ho-ho!' laughed PC Mogpuss, who was wearing a mustard and brown check short single-breasted jacket with a real suede collar and chestnut suede trousers, 'these are just some old things I happened to fling on.'

'Good-oh! I like that!' exclaimed the Duchess, clumping him heartily and dispensing with g's. 'Casual. Shows good breedin'. Well, look. I want to buy a tie for a man. Wondered if you'd help me choose, what?'

This at first threw PC Mogpuss into convulsions of rapture, inlaid with pride that his own tactful treatment was causing this repressed and sensitive soul to speak out; but these were quickly followed by fears that the tie might be for Smith. He knew that women were fatally attracted to worthless scoundrels. He plied her with questions: was the gentleman of a robust appearance? 'No,' replied the Duchess off-handedly, 'undersized little twerp, actually.' Was the gentleman a member of the servant classes? 'Hardly,' said the Duchess. 'He's a curator of somethin' or other.'

'Ah, an academic.' Satisfied that this could not be

Smith, PC Mogpuss led the Duchess into a shop, where she became Miss Hoskyn again. They looked at ties: dark green Liberty print ones, Roman coin ones, red-green paisley ones, navy floral ones, red and white spot ones, burgundy with blue-green floral design ones, navy with large white spot ones, and many more, all silk. Miss Hoskyn shook her head at them all. PC Mogpuss was not used to shopping with women, and began to be disheartened.

'What about a bow tie?' he suggested.

'Ah yes,' exclaimed the Duchess in her normal voice, to the astonishment of the shop-man, 'that's a crackin' good idea!'

'We have this one in wine-red, madam,' he said.

'Yes, I like that,' whispered Miss Hoskyn.

'It is in fact one of our most popular lines,' said the shop-man with renewed enthusiasm. 'It is made up for convenience – '

'Made up?' said the Duchess, at full volume again. 'That's no good.'

At last one was found that had to be tied by digital manipulation, and when they were out of the shop PC Mogpuss deferentially asked the Duchess if made-up bow ties were not considered quite top-drawer among the upper classes?

'I wouldn't know,' said the Duchess. 'This one'll take him longer to tie, that's all. That's what I was lookin' for.'

The Toothpeaces were beginning, unknown to each other, to feel the stirrings of doubt about their intentions. After a few years of marriage each had said, 'I have made a ghastly mistake.' Each now wondered whether the ghastly mistake hadn't been in saying this. Hubert, watching the huge stone pot fall through the air, had felt quite a pang of dismay, and when it knocked the ear off the lion he was sobered by the thought that it would have damaged Angela even more. He realized that he would even miss her cantankerous bickerings over words; he'd got used to them; they supplied a certain need, as roughage does in food. The Duchess's language, on the other hand, was beginning to pall. ('What-ho!' was a vile phrase.) And although he found it pleasant to say things like 'spiffing wheeze' and 'SPLAT!', he didn't want an exclusive diet of them, any more than one wants to eat nothing but roughage.

Angela had similar misgivings. When Hubert, coated with plaster, had contended that soot was not white, she had been quite touched by his impeccable pedantry. Sir John Marvell, on the other hand, was given to some embarrassing excesses. (A dotted line named Habbakuk, forsooth!) She had the additional discomfort of waiting for Hubert to be murdered, and felt uneasy whenever he stood before the wardrobe mirror.

Neither knew that the other was an accomplice to the crime of murder. Incarcerated in their gaol of words, they had no more idea of what was going on in the outside world than has the average lifer. Not only that; they hardly realised what murder implied. One might almost go so far as to say that each expected the other to get up and jump about after the deed, like the characters in animated cartoons.

The Duchess of Sligo had run out of ideas for killing Angela for the moment, but she was still of good cheer, because she was now engrossed in her work as accessary to the murder of Hubert. Was this not defeating her own ends? Yes, but she preferred the chase to the kill, and didn't worry too much about the quarry, so long as there was one. She was pleased with the bow tie, and practised tying it round her own neck to make sure that this took time. Yes, there were no convenient clips or loops; if you hadn't been brought up to wear this sort of thing you might fiddle with it for long minutes. She slipped the word to Hubert that she had bought him a present, and he, under the pretext of searching under the bed for an aphorism, persuaded Angela to go on ahead to the bar.

She went reluctantly, for nowadays she hardly cared to let Hubert out of her sight. She even warned him to take care, although of what she did not say. 'Have no fear; aphorisms are not malignant,' he replied good-temperedly. He was moved by her apparently undue concern, but he was quite childishly excited at the thought of a present, and when the Duchess came in with the wine-red bow tie he was delighted, and began immediately to affix it to his satisfaction. It set off his small, circular face becomingly, but he was as fussy with ties as he was with words, and kept adjusting it, which was exactly as the Duchess had planned.

Angela meanwhile had gone not to the bar but to the sitting-room, empty as yet except for Sir John. Although a master of disguises (Angela had no idea he had been the photographer), he did not so easily disguise his own feelings. He strolled to and fro, to and fro in front of the bell-rope with such a show of nonchalance that she thought he might at any moment begin whistling. She watched him as though he were ping-pong in slow motion.

The Duchess, with her usual splendid carelessness, had leaned her gun on the wall outside Hubert's room. It was loaded with blanks, as she disapproved of damaging property. Happy that Hubert was engrossed in fixing his tie before the wardrobe mirror, she slipped into the corridor and fired it.

The bang, in the vault of the hotel landing, was tremendous. Sir John, below, gave the bell-rope a triumphant tug. Angela stood up with confused feelings. Sir John folded his arms with quiet satisfaction, and the Duchess, above, smiled and made to stroll away.

But at this very moment Mr Glossop came down the corridor on his proprietorial tour of the hotel. He was aghast. Miss Hoskyn was not only carrying a gun, she was firing it right at him! She said cheerfully, 'Don't panic. Blanks, what?' but panic he did. He flung himself panting into the nearest refuge, Hubert's room; he shoved Hubert aside with a babbled injunction; he glared round for a further place of hiding: the wardrobe itself! He sprang on to the spot before the mirror and began easing his shoulders into the wardrobe. It was a tight fit; he was stouter than Hubert.

Angela went briskly from the sitting-room and up the stairs, not bothering to use the lift. One flight of stairs, a landing, then another to the second floor. But halfway up this second flight she met Hubert coming down.

'Oh, Hubert!' She wondered for a moment if he were a ghost. 'You *are* Hubert, aren't you?'

'If I do not usurp myself, I am,' he replied equably. 'I do hope, my dear, that you have not picked up that Smith fellow's habit of shouting aloud at what is plainly evident. It could make for discordant social relationships.'

'*Hubert!* What happened?'

'Ah. Perhaps you heard a bang? It was very loud. It may well have been a firearm being discharged. Immediately afterwards the proprietor of this hotel rushed into our room. He was in a highly excited state. He gibbered – and I say "gibbered" advisedly – "Get out of my way quick." I began to explain that "quick" is not an adverb, and that "quickly" was needed here, but he seemed so agitated that I deemed it wise to let him calm down, and that accounts for my being halfway down this staircase.'

'*Hubert!* What did he do next?'

'He appeared to be trying to burrow into our wardrobe – '

'The *wardrobe*!'

'Really, Angela, this mannerism is becoming tedious – '

Angela stayed no longer, but hurried away to their room, Hubert following in puzzlement.

The wardrobe was a pile of shattered and splintered wood. Mr Glossop was nowhere to be seen. Hubert, and subsequently everyone else, supposed that he had smashed up the wardrobe in an insane frenzy and then bolted. But Angela, pale with horror, knew differently. He had been imploded.

'To begin with, the gun was loaded with blanks,' PC Mogpuss told Mrs Hailstone. (He was wearing a bottle-green high-neck single-breasted jacket with large gilt buttons and red and bottle plaid with floral overprint trousers, which, even at this stressful time, she could not quite ignore.) 'Her intention was clearly harmless. Picture the situation. This nervous, highly sensitive young member of the upper classes is suddenly confronted with a frenzied man bearing down upon her with who knows what intentions? Can you wonder that she accidentally pulls the trigger, or even, in her alarm, pulls it in pure self-defence to warn him?'

Mrs Hailstone conceded that an intended murderer would not use blanks, but was otherwise not convinced. However, she was still reluctant to make a fuss. The residents of the Ariel Hotel were pleased to ignore untoward occurrences, but only up to a point. If there were too much adverse publicity they would choose to ignore the hotel itself. The Ariel was Mr Glossop's proud monument and his livelihood, and she would be doing him no service by causing it to be boycotted. Softly-softly was the way.

'What about Mr Glossop?' she said.

'I suspect that he was under the influence of drink.'

'He is a teetotaller.'

'Then he may be insane. I shall watch Miss Hoskyn more closely than ever. We cannot allow a delicately nurtured young woman to be menaced by a maniac.'

'Yes, do that,' said Mrs Hailstone.

Was she being irresponsible? She could not take

the alarming events of the past few days altogether seriously. She was almost as off-hand about them as Mr Norval himself. Something, the vaguest of premonitions, told her that in time the play-acting would stop, that something real and dangerous would threaten and that she and her aids would need to rush to it like firemen to a blaze: but not yet. She hoped, meanwhile, that Mr Glossop had used up all his energy smashing up the wardrobe and was now in retreat somewhere, sleeping it off.

Harriet, heavy of heart and incidentally alliterative, was vacuum-cleaning the second-floor corridor. She did not doubt that Mavis was treating the 'grave responsibility' of Norman's infatuation with all the gravity of a seductive squirrel. Her pretty hesitations and reluctance, in fact, would only arouse him further. And as for beating their detective team at their own game, what chance did she herself really stand? How could she begin? In Mavis's favourite stories the private detective was either famous before the tale began, and consulted by forelock-touching police, or else so socially eminent (monocled Lord Percy and his kind) that he was deferred to by all. Harriet herself was a room-maid, the lowliest person in the hotel. How could she question people, study evidence, follow up clues? Her position was hopeless. She switched off the vacuum-cleaner and stood forlorn.

The hum of the cleaner was followed by the usual cathedral hush of the great hotel; but this was broken by a scratching and scraping noise. It seemed to come from a nearby store-room. Harriet looked at the door uneasily. She thought of rats – and she was squeamish about rats. She made one or two snatches at the door-handle without touching it; then she summoned up her courage and with a sudden jerk pulled the door wide.

It was not rats, but Mr Glossop, sprawling on the floor, elaborately involved with the store-room paraphernalia.

With his fat round face, protruding eyes, and his parted and trembling lips, he looked like an oversized baby. He stared at Harriet for several seconds before saying, in a childish falsetto:

'Reggie Glossop is a sausage.'

9

Angela was indignant. She had never whole-heartedly agreed to Hubert's murder in the first place, and now, being a woman of high principles, she deplored the annihilation of an innocent hotel proprietor. Besides, the thing could hardly remain a secret, and she could see that she might in time be implicated, and even sent to prison. She rounded on Sir John Marvell.

'You have been grossly incompetent!'

Sir John was nettled, all the more so because his experiment had not been a complete success. The wardrobe should have remained intact, not been blown to pieces. All the same, his main object had been achieved: the inmate of the wardrobe had been imploded.

'But it was *the wrong man*,' insisted Angela, her voice cracking on a high note.

'Surely you can see that that is irrelevant?'

'So it is irrelevant if soldiers shoot their own men instead of the enemy?'

'The man forced his way into the wardrobe, usurping its intended occupant. I cannot be held responsible for the actions of a lunatic.'

'Oh yes you can, and will be, by the police!'

'Have no fear on that account. The world has not yet caught up with my genius. Everyone assumes that Glossop smashed the wardrobe up in some insane paroxysm. We shall let them think so. In a way I am glad this has happened, because I admit the thing could have been done more neatly. I shall make some slight adjustments, and next time it will work perfectly.'

'You can make all the adjustments you like if it passes the time for you,' said Angela, 'but there won't be a next time.'

'You reject all my proposals!' said Sir John angrily.

'I only wish I had!'

'Have a care, Angela. This is tantamount to rejecting *me*.'

'Ah,' said Angela ominously, 'I was coming to that.'

More disappointment would have been heaped on Sir John had he known that implosion, as he termed it, had not taken place at all; or at any rate there had been far more *ex* than *im*. True, Mr Glossop had been relatively unharmed, which is unusual in these cases, but otherwise everything had blown to bits in the most conventional manner. The wardrobe was a pile of matchwood, and a hole had been blown in the floor of the Toothpeaces' room and the ceiling of the store room, and through it Mr Glossop fell to an entanglement with brooms, buckets, bottles of detergent, and coils of flex of indeterminate purpose. He was more shocked than hurt, although he did sustain one or two nasty bruises and lay for a while in a daze. He was convinced, however, that he had been shot and had died. So strong was this conviction that, as he lay crumpled in the dark storeroom, all his past life unreeled itself before his eyes. Most of it was pretty boring and doesn't bear recording – he saw himself poring over books, taking examinations, being awarded certificates and stuff like that – but one picture kept coming round again, like a programme in the cinema. A ring of squeaky little girls danced round him with their eyes crossed and their tongues hanging out. They cackled derisively. At first Mr Glossop took them for minor demons and was appalled to think where he had ended up. Then, dimly, he recognized them. He heard their words, which rose tremulously to his own lips. And then, as in his horrified mind he faced an eternity of this torment, he was reprieved: a door opened, light poured in, and he saw an angel.

This in a sense was literally true, for it is a known fact that women become ministering angels when pain and anguish wring the brow; but Harriet looked the part as well. She was wearing a freshly-laundered white house-coat; her fair hair rippled about her shoulders and a tendril of it touched her cheek; and her face, softened in shadow as she looked into the store-room, was filled with such tender concern that it melted the heart to see her. Her hands, as she extricated Mr Glossop from mops and buckets and discreetly felt his person for broken bones, tended him like a caress. He had half-decided that Heaven was a store-room and that here he would dwell in bliss, couched among the domestic utensils for the rest of time, when she said, 'Try to stand up, sir. Lean on me. There,' and wrapping his arm round her shoulders, and circling his waist, she conducted him into the corridor.

He recognized her now: she was not exactly an angel, but as good as; she was the beautiful girl on whom he had thrown strange regards ever since her arrival. She was involved, somehow, with his own destiny.

This was the first time, incredibly, that he had ever submitted to the embrace of a woman, and although his terror of women rose in him even as he did so, he felt with a pang that a woman, one woman, *the* woman, could also be his salvation, expelling his complex as fire drives out fire, or one nail knocks out another.

The incident brought out the best in Harriet, but at the same time she determined to make the most of it. She felt that she had landed herself a prize. She knew that Norman Norval had first come here on Mr Glossop's account, and she was not above hoping that here at last was her chance to get ahead of him. She naturally supposed Mr Glossop to be involved in a plot in which, in fact, the poor man had no part whatever, and she intended to keep him to herself. (Do even real angels, one wonders, feel jealous ever? Do they resent interference?)

She would not allow him to use the lift, for fear that someone else might enter it, but persuaded him that it was better for him to walk. She escorted him to the third floor and through the door marked 'Private: Staff Only', and into his office. She lowered him into his leather-padded revolving chair and sat opposite him. She rested her arms on his desk and leaned forward.

'Tell me everything, sir,' she said.

The pair had not entirely escaped notice, however. As they turned the stairs at the end of the second corridor, the Toothpeaces came out of their room and spotted them. Angela's reaction was alarming. She pointed a trembling finger at Mr Glossop's back.

'The proprietor!'

'Oh, my dear, *really!*' protested Hubert. This exclamatory habit of hers was getting worse. He foresaw the time when she would do nothing but shriek continually at random objects. But Angela tottered back into their room and sank on to the bed, white-faced.

'He is alive!'

'That is indubitable,' said Hubert.

'And so are you!'

'Yes, but that is not a matter for astonishment.'

'It is more so than you think,' said Angela, and burst into tears.

Hubert's heart stirred. Angela was no longer willowy, wilting, nor even noticeably flexible; she was shaken by real feelings, shedding real tears. It came home to him that he did not want her poisoned with weedkiller, nor yet shattered by a huge stone pot dropped from a height.

He wanted her alive, he wanted her all in one piece, he wanted *her*. Awkwardly, for he was at home with words, not gestures, he pulled her hands from her face.

'Come now, the fact that I am alive is nothing to cry about.' Then suddenly the strange events of the past few days sprang to his mind, and he was assailed by doubts. 'Is it?'

She stood up, pale and trembling.

'Hubert, I have something to tell you.'

It had already dawned on him what it was. He felt a rush of fellow-feeling for her. To want to murder him implied a force of emotion which could not express itself in disputes over orifices and egresses. It meant that he *mattered* to her. By the same token, she mattered to him. Each man kills the thing he loves. Or better still, tries to and misses. He looked at her with great earnestness.

'Equally, I have something to tell you.'

'No, I object to *equally*,' said Angela, with some of the old pedantry. 'This is most important.'

'So is this.'

'We cannot speak simultaneously.'

Hubert hesitated, then bowed.

'True,' he said courteously. 'Ladies first.'

In faltered mutterings, punctuated by silences which a writer would represent by a line of dots, Mr Glossop exposed to Harriet the history of the squeaky little girls and the trauma they had caused. She nodded sympathetically. Such a thing was enough to put a man off women and sausages for life. But what help was there? Would merely talking do? Diagnosis was not a cure in itself.

Oh heavens, she thought, seeing the expression on Mr Glossop's face, he thinks he sees the answer in *me*. One of the drawbacks of being a beautiful girl was that you hardly dared to be nice to anyone. They took it too personally. All she could do would be to lead him on until his imaginary tragedy became a real one.

She excused herself eventually on the grounds of her duties and reported Mr Glossop's reappearance to Mrs Hailstone, omitting to mention the time she had spent talking to him. Mrs Hailstone hurried to him with such alacrity that Harriet stood in the corridor awhile in speculation, as the possibility of another solution entered her mind.

Then she remembered Norman's obscure remark: 'It's not the past that matters, it's our memory of the past.' That, in the light of Mr Glossop's revelations, now made sense. And suddenly she decided not to go on alone any longer. What she now knew would matter to Norman. A cynic might decide that she had seen a means of getting back to him, but Harriet did not think that way at all; she saw it as her duty to break their silence. He did not deserve it, but she would. So dutiful did she feel that her heart beat faster.

(Moreover she knew a lot more than Mavis did, detective's assistant or not.)

She fluttered about, carrying out her duties, but hastening every two or three minutes to the second floor, hiding in and out of rooms, until Norman appeared and entered his room.

And now an awful shyness overtook her. She walked irresolutely about the corridor.

Some other time, perhaps, not now?

What was she to say if she went in?

Suppose he didn't say anything, but just gave her that sleep-walking stare?

She edged nearer and nearer to his door. Her knees all but gave way. Then she threw open his door and went in.

'When Mr Glossop was five years old he was teased by some little girls who said he was a sausage. That's why he hates his name. And sausages. And women. The little girls will be about fifty now but he hasn't forgotten them. I mean, he had until he had a shock and remembered. He was in the store-room below this floor. And another thing: Mr Smith fixed up something in the wardrobe. In the Toothpeaces' room I mean. He couldn't have been after Mr Glossop. Must be the Toothpeaces. Only Mr Glossop fell through the floor . . .'

While she was speaking Norman stood up, came slowly towards her, took her by the wrists, then the elbows, then the shoulders, and finally became as much entangled with her as Mr Glossop had been with the paraphernalia in the store-room.

'I've thought of nothing but you,' he said. 'All day long, every day. Anything I've done or said has been just going through the motions. I haven't slept a wink, but when I have I've dreamed of you. I haven't moved anything in this room because your hands have touched it all. I love you. I worship you. I've even thought I'd die for love of you but where would be the point, I'd only go on adoring you beyond the grave. You must be quite heartless or you'd know all this.'

'Why have you been such a pig?' said Harriet.

'I will accept that your first failure was sheer misfortune,' said Hubert, 'but to fail a second time looks like inefficiency.'

'Just rotten luck, Hube. Could happen to the best of us. Better luck next time, what?'

'What means do you intend to employ?'

'Not sure. I still rather favour shootin' her.'

'Did you not nearly succeed in shooting the proprietor of this hotel? I understand that he is still in a state of shock.'

'The chump kept gettin' in the way. Still, we'll try some other way if you like. Got any ideas?'

'As a matter of fact, yes. I suggest we drop the plan altogether.'

'What?'

'I must explain, Amanda, that my feelings for my wife

have changed. She has shown me some quite moving solicitude of late. Moreover, she has revealed a surprising depth of emotion. I have reason to believe that she even wanted to kill me. And of course she expresses herself admirably. Admittedly, I question her terminology at times, but generally speaking – '

'*Hubert!*' exclaimed the Duchess, with a blackening brow, 'just what the hell are you sayin'?'

'You did not let me finish. Generally speaking, I find that she is superior to yourself.'

'To *me*?' shouted the Duchess. 'She's middle class, dammit. She's – she's *suburban!*'

'It is not that I do not appreciate the sacrifices you have made on my account,' said Hubert, 'but I must express my feelings roundly. You have an amusing way of speaking, but I find that it palls with repetition. Did you know, by the way, that you never sound the letter "g" at the end of a word?'

Now, the Duchess had lost her appetite for Hubert of late – it will be remembered that she had recently referred to him as 'an undersized little twerp' – and it would not have upset her much to give him up, but that *he* should give *her* up aroused in her all the fury of a woman scorned. She glared at him, speechless.

'I am sure that you will understand,' said Hubert, 'that when it comes to making a choice, Angela is the obvious one.'

The Duchess was a basilisk, but Hubert hardly noticed. He was too occupied in congratulating himself on his phrasing. It had been lucid without hyperbole or rodomontade. He bowed politely and left the room.

Did smoke pour from the Duchess's nostrils? She stood for a while snorting and pawing the ground, and then stormed into the corridor.

Here she encountered PC Mogpuss, who, impressed by the bow tie she had bought, was wearing a burgundy silk paisley one of his own, with a wine-striped shirt and matching silk braces with leather ends. He halted before her, looking concerned.

'Madam, I can't help noticing that you look very distressed. Forgive me for asking, but has that fellow been upsetting you?'

He meant Mr Smith, of course, but the Duchess's mind was full of Hubert.

'Upsettin' me? He's got me hoppin' mad!'

She raged on out of sight. PC Mogpuss set his jaw. He'd catch that Smith fellow out sooner or later, and then wouldn't he deal with him! He went his way, looking more like a resolute Boy Scout than ever, albeit at the same time repeating to himself the term Miss Hoskyn had just used. 'Hoppinmad.' It had an upper-class ring. He would cultivate it.

The Duchess strode out of the hotel, gave St Phocas and the marble lady a glare in passing that might well have turned them to stone, had they not been safe in that element already, and crashed her way into the wood with the intention of easing her feelings by uprooting a few trees. Approaching the familiar clearing, however, she observed that the air was shimmering as if in a heat haze, and there, sitting on the log, grinding his teeth, was Sir John Marvell. At first they glared at each other fiercely, hung over with rage; but the harmony that always existed between them prevailed, and both were almost instantly soothed by the balm of friendship.

'I could kill that Hubert,' said the Duchess, sitting beside him.

'Ha!' said Sir John. 'Our positions have become reversed.'

And they exchanged confidences. Each was indignant for the sake of the other at the perfidy of the Tooth-peaces, man and wife.

'I never really hated that droopin' jonquil till now,' said the Duchess. 'I mean, no hard feelin's. She just had to be got rid of, that's all. But this is somethin' else. I mean, treatin' you like this. It's just not on.'

'My sentiments exactly,' said Sir John. 'I bore Tooth-peace no ill-will. He was just an insipid object to be eliminated. But now that the pride of a friend has been wounded, he has incurred my deadliest wrath.'

And the class sentiments, always so strong a force in the English character, rose up in these two and set them ablaze with indignation. She was a Duchess and he a knight, and they had been spurned by commoners. By commoners.

'Well,' said Sir John thickly, 'all one can do now is leave them to stew in their own juice.'

'Absolutely,' said the Duchess.

They sat silent for a while, amicable in their injured pride.

'After all we've done for them,' said the Duchess. 'Especially you, Sir John. Your inventions could've won prizes.'

'Oh, you too, Duchess. Your scaling of the hotel roof was a breathtaking feat.'

Another silence.

'Pity all that effort has to be wasted,' remarked the Duchess at last.

'It is indeed.'

'Oh dammit,' exclaimed the Duchess, 'do we *have* to give it up? I mean, we've helped each other pretty well already, what? But if we were a proper team, instead of doin' this turn-and-turn-about lark, we'd really show 'em, what?'

'There is no doubt they deserve to die,' said Sir John slowly.

'So they do. And you know, I've never liked givin' up a chase once I've started. Not my style.'

'You would give heart to any man,' said Sir John admiringly. 'What are the words to that fine old song? "From a find to a check" . . .'

' – from a check to a view,' added the Duchess, her eyes lighting up at the noble words.

'From a view to a kill,' completed Sir John with murderous satisfaction.

Much cheered by this pleasant chat, they began strolling back to the hotel.

'I wish I'd seen him when the plaster fell on him,' remarked the Duchess. 'Must have been a hoot.'

'Yes, he looked like a grotesque statue. It's a pity the plaster didn't fall on her as well.'

'Then they'd have looked like two statues,' chortled the Duchess. 'Stand-ins for those two fellers, what?'

They were just passing the niche house.

'Yes,' said Sir John, and halted. He looked long and hard at St Phocas and his companion. 'Yes, indeed,' he said.

He turned back to the Duchess. They looked at each other with a wild surmise.

10

Norman Norval's gift had forced him to lead a protected life. At school he passed all his exams easily, getting 100 per cent in all of them, because he knew all the questions before the examiners had thought of them and the answers before he had read the questions. Consequently, he sailed through school and university unaware of the struggles that the rest of us have to endure. The private company of Paranoics Anonymous took him on readily and paid him highly, and at first he got on comfortably enough, assuming a deep and treacly voice and telling clients what they wanted to know. Before long, however, he realized that his gift was more nuisance than it was worth. For one thing, it deprived him of hope, because hope can only exist where there is doubt. For another, it offered him worldly success without having to work for it, and he was wise enough to know that that threatened disaster. As he grew older, he wished to lose his gift altogether. You think he was ready to throw a pearl away? A millstone, rather. The greatest blessing is to be like everyone else.

When he came to the Ariel, complications upset his simple system.

The Toothpeaces. He knew that they wanted each other murdered. But at the same time, they *didn't* want it, and the future, which Norman had always found predictable, hung in the balance.

Sir John Marvell and the Duchess. An odd case. They wanted to commit murder, and were trying hard to do so, but for mistaken motives. They thought they wanted to marry Angela and Hubert respectively. They didn't. And so their will was impaired by a curious reluctance. And where the will was impaired, things just wouldn't happen, however much they tried. That was why the sherry wasn't poisoned, Sir John couldn't implode Doctor Toothpeace, and Angela wasn't clobbered by the huge stone pot. For things, Norman discovered to his amazement – i.e. huge stone pots, wardrobes, etc. – were actually at the command of the human will.

There was something else. If Sir John and the Duchess managed to get rid of their mistaken motives, a real force of will would overtake the charade and they would commit murder successfully. This knowledge, a black cloud, had hung in Norman's mind ever since his arrival. That was why he had been staring at ceilings and babbling like some crazy oracle about St Phocas and the marble woman.

There was yet something else. Norman had fallen in love. This was a demented condition that led him to make confusing statements, such as that he hadn't slept a wink and yet kept dreaming. It baffled his wits even further.

Harriet was being most understanding. She agreed, however reluctantly, that he would be better off without his gift. How could he get rid of it? Not by a surgical operation, of course. By psychological means, then.

It had something to do with his name, but what she was unable to decide.

She herself was discovering that every asset is in some way a liability. Simply by being Harriet Gardiner she had won the regard of two men. Because of this she had antagonized two women.

Outwardly, both Mrs Hailstone and Mavis were being nice to her. Terribly nice. So nice that they might have been made of cake. Their niceness made her feel awful. Yet what had she done? She felt guilty for no other reason than for being herself.

Mrs Hailstone said, 'Mr Glossop wants you, Harriet.'

'Me?'

'You, dear. You and no other. You really have got them dropping by the wayside, haven't you, Harriet?' She looked at Harriet's rueful face and laughed. 'Oh, don't look like that!' she said. 'Be glad you've got so much going for you. There ought to be a law against it, but still. Go on, go and practise your art.' And she gave Harriet a friendly little smack and hustled her out.

Mrs Hailstone had reason to feel slighted, because she had cared for Mr Glossop and his interests with the devotion of a Samaritan.

She believed, of course, that it was he who had smashed up the Toothpeaces' wardrobe, and ripped up the floor beneath it and flung himself to the floor below. It was an inefficient method of committing suicide, but she decided that this was just another sign of his madness, which was beginning to take a violent form. Supremely anxious to protect his hotel from scandal and loss of guests, she hurried him off to bed and called a doctor, to whom she said nothing of his insanity, merely explaining that he had had a fall. The doctor declared that Mr Glossop had mild concussion, prescribed rest and some pills, and went his unsuspecting way. Mrs Hailstone now prepared to nurse Mr Glossop night and day, and do her own work at odd moments.

Mr Glossop asked to see Harriet. Indeed he demanded to see Harriet. Resignedly, Mrs Hailstone saw to it that he did see Harriet, and confirmed her conviction that there was no justice in the world.

Her only consolation was that the Toothpeaces were being wonderfully good-natured about the further destruction of their room. They would not hear of being given a new one, not even the luxurious bridal suite. The floor having been mended and a new wardrobe supplied, they were perfectly happy with the one they had. Mrs Hailstone made a note to cancel their bill.

When she had gone they looked at each other in relief and satisfaction.

'I am glad that the matter has ended as it has,' said Angela.

'Yes,' said Hubert. 'Let me say that I feel I went too far. To contrive your actual demise was, I admit, excessive.'

'I am equally to blame,' said Angela.

'Our experience,' said Hubert, 'should be a lesson to all against intemperance and excess.'

'Yes indeed,' said Angela. 'One should remember to exercise moderation in all things, especially when one goes to extremes. One thing still puzzles me. Whatever did I see in Sir John Marvell, alias Smith?'

'Or I in the Duchess,' agreed Hubert, 'and to be frank, it is hard to see what those two saw in us. Do you not agree?'

'I do, and I also concur.'

'Both matches were impossible,' said Hubert. But he checked himself. 'No, that puts it, I think, a little too strongly. Incredible? No, no. Preposterous? There again, that is not quite right.'

Angela suggested tentatively, 'Improbable?'

'What?' demanded Hubert eagerly.

'Improbable?' faltered Angela.

'Yes! Oh yes! Improbable! the very word!'

'You really think so?' said Angela, blushing with pleasure.

'Oh yes! Oh Angela, my love, what should I do

without you and your impeccable diction? There is, after all, no one like you!'

He enfolded her in his arms. She rested her chin on the top of his head.

Harriet was directed to Mr Glossop's bedroom, where she found him lying amid lemon-coloured silk sheets. She was apprehensive as to what duties were expected of her, but he just heaved himself up against a pile of pillows and talked. And talked and talked.

She found that he did not require answering, but burbled away in a semi-trance. He generated pathos, and for a while Harriet felt sorry for him in a patronizing way, as though he were senile and she the matron of an old folks' home. But she was too sensible to feel like this for long, and soon his great merits occurred to her: he must have a fine business head and an enormous capacity for work, and as a matter of fact, if he lost a couple of stone, he wouldn't be bad-looking either, with his squat square body and bullet head. Quite a Napoleonic figure, in fact. But meanwhile he fastened his melancholy eyes on her and burbled.

The squeaky little girls, identifying him with a sausage, occupied a lot of his burble. But then the little girls grew up, and his talk became infested with menacing shapes like vampires. He did not describe their appearance, but Harriet formed the impression of white-faced creatures in dark glasses, with cruel mouths and glistening blood-red lips. They were very tall and thin, and they drifted forward in wreaths of white mist. Harriet grew quite scared of the picture she had conjured up, and lost any inclination to laugh at him.

She listened. And listened and listened, until he fell asleep, and Mrs Hailstone came in and settled him down among his pillows.

'Well, Harriet, have you uttered the magic words?'
'I haven't uttered anything much, just listened.'

'Ah. So some more sessions are to take place, are they?'

'I don't know. Maybe.'

'I thought they might.'

Those simple words were loaded with inference. Harriet felt uncomfortable and resentful.

Norman had once said that putting Mr Glossop right would be quite a little thing, like putting a fuse in a plug. Well, Norman was the star of Paranoics Anonymous. And Mr Glossop was assuredly paranoid. So Norman should come up with something. Never mind mad detective and his girl assistant. Let him do his job.

'No, listen, Norman,' she said, fending him off, for nowadays he was wont to fasten on her like steel on a magnet, 'your professional services are required.' She gave him a neat précis of Mr Glossop's burblings.

'Yes,' said Norman. 'If he could believe he was someone else he'd come to himself.'

'Norman, that's a paradox and rather irritating.'

'It's a fact. You've said it yourself. It's his name. That's the simple little thing that could make all the difference. If he could change his name and believe in the new one he'd be cured. But the trouble with neurotics is they love their neuroses. It'd be like telling a drunk that all he needed to do was stop drinking. He wants to lose his name, but at the same time he's scared stiff of doing so.'

'He's in a right fix,' sighed Harriet, foreseeing more 'sessions', and Mrs Hailstone's deepening disapproval.

'Yes, glued to Glossop.'

'Women change their names when they marry,' reflected Harriet.

'That wouldn't help Mr Glossop,' said Norman. 'To have a Mrs Glossop around would only make things twice as bad.'

Harriet had a momentary vision of the vampire women, all called Glossop, with necklaces of sausages, but she ordered this sternly from her mind and directed it to Mrs Hailstone. Surely that was where his rescue lay? But what help was there if he couldn't see it?

Harriet, having secured Norman, now saw Mavis in quite a different light. Mavis was no longer a dangerous sex kitten. Mavis, Harriet decided with compassion, was fated to be a friendly girl but never a girlfriend. She was pretty, she was fun, but something indefinable was lacking in her. Perhaps it was that you couldn't take her seriously? You couldn't imagine Norman – or anyone – telling Mavis soulfully that he hadn't moved the things in his room because her hands had touched them. She would probably giggle, ruining the effect of that beautiful speech. Love is sombre. Yet Mavis was terribly romantic. Look at her wistful longing for 'cosy' murders. Harriet was so sorry for her that tears came into her eyes, all the more pitiful because she felt herself partly to blame.

It was Mavis's turn to bring in the cocoa. She sat on Harriet's bed and talked so jauntily and laughed so merrily that you could see she was unhappy. Harriet longed to put her arms round her, to comfort her, to console her. She knew what to say. Norman? Oh, he was all right for a certain type of girl, but not for Mavis. Too intense altogether. Mavis needed a happy extrovert like herself. And there were hundreds just waiting to be had – oh yes there were, darling, they'd be queueing round the block for her, she'd see . . . Harriet had not told Mavis how things stood between Norman and herself, and so she supposed that Mavis didn't know. In fact their love was as obvious as the stone lions out front. However, Harriet couldn't bring herself to embrace her and say all this, and so she too chattered inanely and trilled with false laughter.

Then Mavis said suddenly, 'I've put Norman off, Harriet. I had to.'

'Have you, Mavis?'

'Well, it was getting a bit embarrassing. I didn't want to give him the wrong idea. It wouldn't be fair to my fiancé.'

'You're engaged, Mavis?' said Harriet, sitting up straight.

'Didn't you know?'

'You've never told me!'

'I thought everyone knew.'

'What's his name?'

'Er, Rupert.'

'Very nice. What does he do? What's his job?'

'He's, er, he's a trainee manager in Marks and Spencer.'

'A good career! Would that be the Marks and Sparks in the village?'

'Er, no, not in this village, not exactly.'

'Where, then?'

'Oh, he sort of moves around.'

'What, far away?'

'That's right,' said Mavis, and added with inspiration, 'that's why he doesn't call for me, see?'

'Well, it's wonderful news, Mavis darling,' said Harriet heartily.

'Yes, well, you can see why I have to keep Norman at arms' length, can't you? It wouldn't be fair to Robert.'

'I thought you said his name was Rupert.'

'Oh. Oh yes, yes, it is. Rupert Robert. Some call him one and some the other.'

'What's his surname?'

Mavis was being rushed too fast for plausible invention. 'Roberts,' she stammered.

This was getting too much like third degree, Harriet decided. She congratulated Mavis with overacted enthusiasm and chattered further and laughed to near hysteria until they parted. Then she lay in the dark and shed a few tears. She liked Mavis more than ever. She was very moved by her pathetic lies. How sad life was. But all the same, what a compensation to have Norman in tow.

Angela Toothpeace lay awake in the small hours. She had dozed off several times already, but now she had begun questioning herself as to whether her new state of mind could be called *bliss* or *happiness*. One spoke of *a happy marriage*, of course. But people speaking of Heaven told of *everlasting bliss*. It was a pretty point. She was inclined to wake Hubert for his opinion, but decided against it. Then, as she lay cogitating, she thought she heard a noise.

It came from the region of the floor just outside the new wardrobe. She raised herself on her elbow. Her eyes were accustomed to the darkness and she thought she saw a circular section of the floor, about the size of a dustbin lid, rise a few inches into the air. Puzzled, she sat up and pulled the light cord above the bed. This aroused Hubert, who blinked and demanded what was the matter.

'I thought I saw a circular section of the floor, about the size of a dustbin lid, rise a few inches into the air.'

'You were dreaming.'

'No, I have been awake for some time.'

'You had an hallucination,' said Hubert equably.

'No, my mind was quite lucid. I will allow that it might have been an illusion.'

'Let us say, the sensuous perception of an external object involving a false belief,' said Hubert tactfully. 'Shall we go to sleep?'

'Yes, dear,' said Angela, and added, in her new harmony with her husband, 'how well you express it.'

'Thank you, my love.' Hubert settled into sleep again. Angela lay for a while with a little frown knitting her brows. But there, Hubert really had expressed the matter very neatly.

And contented, she too went to sleep.

Sir John Marvell, in the store-room below, gnashed his teeth. Foiled again. Curses. He had intended to hoist himself into the Toothpeaces' room and quietly kill the two of them, but Angela's being awake at such an unreasonable hour had thwarted this. Really, these people had no sense of occasion. Didn't they know there was a time and place for everything?

He had in fact been lucky to escape detection, for Hubert's words on waking had distracted Angela's attention and allowed him to lower the dustbin-lid-sized section of floor unobserved. But we seldom acknowledge our good fortune, and Sir John left the store-room and went to his bed in a thoroughly bad temper.

11

'I do have the devil's own luck,' grumbled Sir John.

'Well, actually,' said the Duchess, 'it may be just as well you couldn't go ahead with it, old pal. I mean, full marks for compoundin' a subtle poison that kills instantly and leaves no trace, but what about transportin' the bodies? Might run into someone on the way, what? Someone's always about in a hotel.'

'Yes, I admit I was hasty,' muttered Sir John. 'I have so much on my mind at present.'

'So you have,' agreed the Duchess feelingly. She was more sympathetic to Sir John than she had ever been to any living creature, including even her favourite horse.

He was certainly busy. He intended to replace the statues of St Phocas and the marble woman with the petrified bodies of Angela and Hubert. First, he had to carry away the statues and bury them in the wood. The reader who is interested in weight-lifting may care to know that in picking up each statue Sir John would come very near to breaking the world's dead-lift record, but this was no problem to one of his Herculean strength. The bodies themselves would present a greater difficulty. Hubert and Angela did not look exactly like their stone counterparts. Sir John therefore intended to make casts of St Phocas and his companion, each being in two halves like the sarcophagi in some Egyptian tombs, and to seclude Hubert and Angela within them, like the kernels of nuts.

This scheme would add Angela and Hubert to the unsolved cases of missing persons of which our police files are unfortunately full. But many other details had to be attended to first. The new casts would look clean and white, and might be noticed even by the ancient gardener, who could read only with glasses. Then again the original statues would be missing for a while with nothing in their place. Sir John proposed to overcome both these problems by leaving a notice, *'Removed for renovation'* in front of the niche house, and then no one would be surprised when the statues came back fresh and new. This would also salve his conscience, for the placard would be telling the truth, and he was a man of firm principles.

There were other matters to attend to. Sir John had to master the rudiments of sculpture and modelling, and had already got several books on these subjects from the library. He had also decided (with propriety) to embalm the bodies, and was studying that subject too.

But the most elementary difficulty remained the greatest one. How and where was he to inject the Toothpeaces with his untraceable poison?

He left the Duchess's room and went slowly downstairs, black-browed in thought. PC Mogpuss, casually attired in a Loden green reefer jacket with paisley half-lining and an Aran crew-neck sweater, was crouching behind a replica of a George III mahogany long-case clock (with moon-phase aperture). He saw Sir John's scowl and, as the door opened, he caught a glimpse of the worried look on the Duchess's face, and he noted both grimly.

As Sir John prowled across the foyer he saw Mavis at the reception desk, holding up a paperback before her face. It was entitled *Dart of Death*, and the cover showed a sinister-looking monkey holding a blowpipe to its lips, crouching behind a man in evening-dress. The latter was levelling a revolver at a monocled man who had his hands up but wore a mocking smile.

Sir John did not waste courtesy on hotel employees. 'Show me that book, Miss,' he commanded.

Mavis, in no mood for cheek from anyone, looked up glaring, but when she saw who it was a gleam came into her eye. She handed him the book without a word. He read at the opened page:

> 'The game's up, Wimpish.'
>
> 'On the contrary, Carruthers,' drawled Lord Percy, 'it's up for you, old fruit. I think I ought to mention that a sinister-looking monkey is crouchin' behind you holdin' a blowpipe to its lips.'
>
> 'You think you can catch me with that old trick, you fool . . .'
>
> There was a f-f-f-t! from the pipe. Carruthers slumped.
>
> 'You should have heeded your Uncle Percy, old egg . . .'

Sir John did not bother to find out whether Lord Percy grappled with the monkey or shook hands with it. He had had an idea. He ejaculated 'Ha!', tossed the paperback on to Mavis's desk, and strode out full of purpose.

Mavis's eye was still gleaming. She had just observed Mr Smith showing great interest in a method of killing. Norman Norval would surely be impressed with this piece of evidence.

And correspondingly grateful to her.

She was not a girl to give up lightly, nor did she think any battle lost until it was won.

One antiques shop in the high street of Mockery Hollow was devoted entirely to weapons and the accoutrement of battle. It was stacked with every kind of firearm as well as shields, casques, whole suits of armour for man and horse, swords, daggers, spears, halberds and spiked metal balls that swung on chains. One small room was given up to sword sheaths (ivory); another to assegais, tomahawks, boomerangs and other primitive weapons. Sir John Marvell had glanced at this last before. He remembered seeing a small, dark, highly-glazed figure in composition, holding a twelve-inch blowpipe to its face.

He now examined this and found that the blowpipe could be detached, leaving a hole in the manikin's fist. The shop-man, however, would not let him buy it separately.

'Afraid not, sir,' he said apologetically. 'He'd be lost without it. I couldn't be so cruel.'

'So I've got to buy the whole thing?'

'Afraid so, sir.'

So Sir John did so, and lugged it back to the hotel. The shop-man, delighted to be rid of a cheap little fake in awful taste, put a large sum of money into his till and remarked to himself that in this trade you never knew your luck.

Norman Norval was rather like those historians who reply 'not my period' when you ask them anything about the past. There was an unlimited lot of future, and he couldn't foretell it all at once. He was always delighted, therefore, when someone filled him in with a bit of information he hadn't had time to foresee. When Mavis told him about Sir John's interest in blowpipes he was so pleased that he kissed her.

Then he immediately apologized. 'I'm so sorry,' he said. 'I forgot myself.'

'How soon will you forget yourself again?' said Mavis, lifting up her innocent face.

This bit of flirting was a tonic he needed. His standards were exceptionally high for our casual times, perhaps because he saw better than others the dangers of being lax, and besides, he had given his heart to Another; but the awful gravity of all this did put him in need of some light relief. He looked down at Mavis appreciatively.

'If it will make you feel better,' she said, 'we'll make it quits,' and kissed him lightly on the cheek. A peck, merely. But no, a peck suggests a beak, and her lips were as soft as the petal of a flower.

'Now what do we do?' demanded Mavis, cheerfully businesslike. 'Clap him on the shoulder and say "The game's up, Smith"?'

'It isn't up yet, and when it is the police will have to do that, not us.'

'You don't mean our resident plain-clothes detective? (Ha, plain clothes, that's a laugh!) Norman, he's the thickest!'

'He'll be in at the finish.'

'Oh, you mean you'll say, "Take him away, Officer," and Mogpuss's bit will just be to put the handcuffs on him?'

'No, he's got a much bigger role than that.'

'Well, you could have fooled me.' Mavis turned to go about her duties. For a fraction she considered kissing him again, but let it pass. He wouldn't have stopped me, though, she told herself.

She met Harriet on the first floor corridor.

'Hallo, Mavis,' said Harriet, very kindly.

'Hallo sweetie!' sang out Mavis.

'She's very cheerful this morning,' observed Harriet, and (for all her affection for Mavis) her spirits clouded very slightly.

Harriet was like St Augustine, who asked the Lord to give him chastity and continency, but not yet. She meant to help Norman get rid of his too-exacting gift, but she had hoped vaguely that one or two dividends might be had from it before he lost it.

But now she felt the need to do him a major service immediately. The matter was urgent.

At lunchtime she shut herself in her room with a sandwich and pondered. She wrote his name, thus:

NORMAN
NORVAL

and then she wrote it thus:

NORVAL
NORMAN

She pondered afresh. Then her face flushed and her heart pounded.

Then misgivings seized her. Could it really be so simple?

But her intuition insisted: yes, yes, names were all-important. That 'what's in a name?' thing of Juliet's was wide of the mark. A name could cause the sales of advertised products to boom or slump. A change of name could raise a pop singer from obscurity to fame and fortune. Why, here right at hand, Mr Glossop's fearful hang-up had arisen, like the soldiers from dragons' teeth, from his name. She had the answer in her hands. QED.

If Norman would agree.

She cut the names, Norman Norval, into little squares such as are used in Scrabble, and waylaid him when he returned to his room after lunch.

'Look, Norman.'

And she laid out:

NORMAN NORVAL . . . NORVAL NORMAN

'Now, she said, 'rearrange each pair to make the same single word.'

'You take the V out of the first pair and the N from the second pair or vice versa,' he said.

'That's right. What does that make you?'

'NORMAL.'

'Right.'

He did not, however, cry 'eureka!' nor, (as she had hoped) seize her in his arms. He looked blank.

'Is that it?'

'That's it,' she said, hiding her disappointment, 'only of course you have to work on it. Oh come on, Norman, think of what you tell your Paranoics clients to do. Twenty minutes a day in the privacy of your own home. Repeat to yourself over and over again, "Norman Norval is Normal".' But she found this to be a tongue-twister, and it came out as 'Norvan Norvav is Norvam'. 'Well, anyway,' she amended, 'just shuffle the letters as you did just now and keep saying "I'm Normal".'

'And that will do the trick?'

'Certainly,' said Harriet, resisting the inclination to thump him. 'Say it often enough and you'll believe it, and you are what you think you are.'

'Oh yes? Don't ever tell that to someone with paranoia.'

But Norman, being in love, was anxious to please, and Harriet's will was strong, and he agreed to do what she said. Doubtfully, however. She was burning to convert him and she was vexed. The trouble with making people see the light was just that: making them see it.

Sir John had formulated a new plan. Concealing himself in the wood, he would shoot the Toothpeaces with poisoned darts as they passed on their way to the village, carry their bodies into the wood and cover them with leaves, enbalm them there in his own good time, and transport them to the niche house ready for their encasement.

Although his purpose was very wicked, one must respect his industry. He had already made careful measurements of the statues and had drawn several diagrams. He had laid in a supply of necessary materials. Difficulties did not daunt him. He was content to use the back of the niche house, cramped though it was, as his work-room.

'Transporting the bodies is going to be a minor problem,' he said to the Duchess. 'If I walk out of the wood with one under each arm I shall risk detection.'

'Likewise, transportin' the statues,' observed the Duchess, 'but I can see a way round it. That gardener chappie has got an enormous wheelbarrow. Borrow that. You can hide them under a heap of leaves.'

'The gardener is an obstinate old man and may be awkward.'

'Yes, a cross-grained old goat. Tell you what, I'll get that well-dressed young policeman feller to persuade him. He's on my side.'

'But – '

'Don't worry. Nice lad.'

'What will you say you want the wheelbarrow for?'

'Oh, compost for the window box or somethin'. Let's try out these darts, then.'

Sir John propped up a dartboard on the window ledge. He had made one or two dummy darts to fit the blowpipe, and he inserted one in the end, drew a breath, and blew. His lung capacity was enormous. Nevertheless the dart performed the feeblest of trajectories and fell to the floor in an incompetent manner before reaching the board.

Sir John tried again and again, blowing until his ears cracked, but always with the same inferior result. He examined the blowpipe for flaws. It seemed intact. He took it angrily back to the shop.

'If you want to commit a murder, sir,' said the shopman, a pleasant, humorous man, 'you'd be better off buying one of my battleaxes.'

'It is merely that when I buy something, I expect it to be in working order.'

'But this was never intended to work. The little figure is for ornament only. No, no; for a blowpipe to project a dart with reasonable force, it would have to be about twelve feet long.'

'Twelve feet,' repeated Sir John.

'That's right. Oh I know you read about people in thrillers being bumped off with peashooter-sized blow-pipes, but I'm afraid the authors haven't done their homework.'

'Twelve feet,' said Sir John again.

'For practical use, yes. It would be quite out of proportion on that nice little chap, though. I trust he looks well in your hallway? No, don't tell me, you've put him by the ornamental pond. So much more original than a garden gnome.'

12

True to his word, Norman Norval shuffled the letters of his name and stared at them, but more in doubt than hope. He had done this several times already, like a conscientious yogi, without effect. He stared so hard that the letters became blurred and he thought he might be going into a trance, but when he raised his eyes they became focused again. He opened the newspaper at the sports page and tested himself on the twelve-thirty at Lingfield. His heart jumped slightly, for he had a moment's uncertainty, something that had never happened before, but only for a moment. In his head a horse soon passed the post. It was called Elegant Dancer. He sighed and went back to his shuffling. He rather resented Harriet's saddling him with this futile ritual.

His thoughts turned to Mavis. With horseracing still in mind, he saw her as an outsider who was coming up fast by the rails. Her innocent pleasure in 'cosy' murders was really very endearing. It would be nice to settle down in her make-believe world where he himself was so important in her eyes.

But there, make-believe worlds were his stock-in-trade, and his job was to liberate people from them. Here in the Ariel Hotel everyone seemed to be living in one. Harriet had said that the Ariel was like a dream palace in the clouds. Abandon ye all reality who enter here.

For that matter, Mockery Hollow itself was a nebula of

imaginary values. But in fact the body of the Ariel was hard stone and the soul of Mockery Hollow was hard cash. St Phocas and the lady were hard stone too. And suddenly Norman – how can one put this? – Norman woke up. He saw clearly what had been troubling his mind all along: the connection between the statues and Smith and Hoskyn. The latter were no longer in a 'charade'. Murder had now become a game. Games are played in earnest. The players take them deadly seriously. But the real world of hard stone and hard cash wouldn't see it as a game. It might seem outrageous to want to protect murderers, but as Norman saw it, they were just as much in need of rescue as the Toothpeaces themselves.

Norman shuffled his letters and felt once again that slight tremor of uncertainty, but when he stood up, shaking himself free of their hypnotic effect, he could still see the future, except that the events were blurred. They raced before his eyes like credit titles that roll too quickly up a screen. Back to the future, he said to himself, and smiled wryly at the joke.

In the corridor, as luck would have it, he came upon Mavis. After such heavy thinking she was a nice relief. He put his arm round her small and lissom waist. She looked up at him with mock reproach and said 'You're fickle', but walked two or three paces before decorously unwinding him. He felt guilty and insisted to himself that his love for Harriet was as profound as ever.

For the rest of the day he avoided both girls. In the evening he bought a paper and looked up the twelve-thirty at Lingfield.

(1) Topsy (2) Elegant Dancer (3) Saracen's Head.

'Only *nearly* right,' he said, and felt faint for a moment.

Mr Glossop had now risen from the yellow silk sheets and was cautiously making his way about the hotel. He observed that the staff, especially the female members, avoided him, putting on an air of deeply virtuous preoccupation as soon as they saw him and scuttling away as fast as they could. He had always believed that he had as much cause to avoid women as the male spider had to avoid his own females, and to be frightening them was a new experience, not disagreeable. It had something to do, he told himself, with his fatal charm, and, experimentally, he deliberately broke one or two valuable objects in their vicinity. This made them scuttle faster than ever. At first he enjoyed a wicked sense of power, much as Mr Hyde must have felt on first noticing his ape-like hands. It soon dawned on him, however, that they simply thought he was mad.

This was unfair. He admitted rushing into the Toothpeaces' wardrobe (the woman had fired a gun at him, for heaven's sake!) but he had not smashed it up in a blind frenzy as everyone supposed. There had been some sort of explosion and he had fallen through the floor. But Mrs Hailstone insisted on humouring him and plying him with tranquillizers, and that young woman Harriet Gardiner (whose beauty was more than human) said nothing at all, but just listened, gravely watching him.

This deeply impressed him. Talkative people should realize what strength there is in silence. It can give the impression of profound understanding. Harriet said nothing because she simply didn't know what to say, but the more she remained silent the more Mr Glossop believed that she had the powers of a seer. He was sure that women had serpents coiled in their hearts, but he made one or two exceptions, of which Harriet was the chief. Or if she was a snake, she was of the prophetess kind, like the Pythoness at Delphi.

He grew more and more sure of this. Finally he interrupted his tedious regurgitations to ask her a question. 'Harriet,' he said, 'you understand me, don't you, my dear?'

'I am trying to, sir.'

114

'Come now, don't be too modest. I have felt all along that you have a wonderful insight into my sorrows. Isn't it true that you have a gift for it?'

Harriet's greatest achievement so far was an A in A-Level biology, but she could see that it would be useful to encourage Mr Glossop in his belief, so she answered, with perfect truth, 'Some people say I have, sir,' not adding that 'some people' was confined to Mr Glossop himself.

'Ah yes, then won't you tell me what I should do?'

Harriet hesitated. She would not risk rushing Mr Glossop into a course of action that she thought obvious but might well terrify him and spoil everything. She said guardedly, 'There is Someone, sir, who can change your life.'

A glow came into Mr Glossop's eyes, and Harriet saw that she had disastrously induced him to think that Someone was herself. She said, slowly and with emphasis, 'You have known her for a long time, but you have never realized how much she matters to you.'

She couldn't hint more heavily. Mr Glossop's eyes changed. They now looked like ponds, calm on the surface, underneath which dark mysterious life was undulating.

What she had said was not without effect. Shortly after this, Mrs Hailstone said quietly, 'Harriet.'

She wore a small, curious smile. 'You've gone up in my estimation – I mean higher than ever,' she said. 'Thanks for trying, Harriet.'

'Mrs Hailstone, I haven't actually mentioned your name.'

'Oh no, you're much too discreet. I appreciate that.'

'Er – has Mr Glossop? . . .'

'Let's say he's showing signs.'

'Well, that's marvellous.'

'Oh no,' said Mrs Hailstone, sounding for the moment

like one of the Toothpeaces, ' "marvellous" would be much too strong. Remotely encouraging would be better. I'm only afraid that we both might run into old age before he gets anywhere.'

'It's his name,' said Harriet.

'Yes, exactly. Don't tell me he ought to change it, because that is just what he won't do.'

'I wish I could help.'

'You've done your best. You're a very nice girl.'

'I don't think being nice is enough. I think a cunning, scheming girl would do better.'

'Oh, I think you've got your share of that,' said Mrs Hailstone, laughing, 'and why not if it's in a good cause?'

'Not getting far, though.'

'Perhaps you should scheme a little harder.'

Sir John Marvell realized – the last in the hotel to do so, probably, because he was rather slow on the uptake – that Mr Glossop was still alive. The shock of this can hardly be overstated. In all his life he had been used to triumphant success. He was now experiencing failure after failure. Implosion didn't work. He had lost Angela. His efforts on the Duchess's behalf had come to nothing. His dummy darts fell short. He had all but lost faith in himself.

The Duchess, as usual, consoled him.

'Look on the bright side, old pal,' she said. 'That proprietor feller was innocent. Bad show if innocent people get killed, what?'

'True.'

'Actually,' said the Duchess, 'we owe the feller an apology. He's been told that he smashed that wardrobe up himself. Thinks he went mad. Not nice to think you've gone mad, what?'

'But if we tell him the truth – ' said Sir John uneasily.

'All the same, ought to own up.'

Sir John's admiration for the Duchess and her code

116

increased. He was, however, a businessman. 'We needn't tell him the *whole* truth,' he said.

But he was gentleman enough to carry out her proposal, and the two of them sought out Mr Glossop and cornered him on the third floor. When he saw the Duchess it was as if one of the vampires in his head had materialized. He cowered against the wall, bereft of speech. When she clumped him in her matey fashion he dropped as though pole-axed. They hauled him to his feet with great courtesy and propped him up between them.

'You've got me wrong, friend,' said the Duchess. 'Fact is, my buddy here and I were plannin' to – '

' – carry out a piece of scientific research,' put in Sir John hastily. 'We are – er – scientific researchers. We research scientifically. We are sorry our scientific researching failed. Also, we are sorry that you were rather put about, and we apologize.'

'That's right,' said the Duchess.

'What sort of experiment?' asked Mr Glossop, his lower jaw wobbling.

'Oh, just one in the name of science,' said Sir John.

'Not – not aimed at me?'

'Good heavens no,' said Sir John. He felt this question to be presumptuous.

'No hard feelin's?' said the Duchess.

'Oh no, no hard feelings,' said Mr Glossop wonderingly. He was much impressed. The Duchess had been the embodiment of his fears, and now he knew that she meant him no harm, his fears themselves were undermined.

'I don't know how to thank you,' he said hoarsely.

'No need,' said Sir John dismissively. He did not want to prolong this conversation.

But Mr Glossop was looking timidly for sympathy. 'I still have my problems,' he said in a whisper. 'Sausages. I hate them.'

'I shouldn't eat them, then,' said Sir John brusquely. He had done the right thing, but he was not obliged to gossip with this hotelier person.

'It's my name,' said Mr Glossop, almost inaudibly, clinging pathetically to this new-found friendship. 'I don't like it.'

'I should change it, then,' said Sir John, positively coldly. And he and the Duchess nodded and walked away, leaving Mr Glossop cheered and yet humiliated.

Sir John went once more to the man who sold weapons.

'Twelve-foot blowpipes?' said the shop-man. 'What a pity. I had one a week ago. Snapped up at once, I'm afraid.'

'Can you get another?'

'Very difficult. The blowpipe as a weapon is sadly neglected.'

'Because it's so difficult to use, no doubt.'

'You've been studying the subject?' asked the shop-man with interest.

'Yes,' said Sir John, 'and I have come to this conclusion: the principle is that the volume of gas inside the pipe expands, fills the pipe, and exerts enough pressure to expel the dart. The pipe must be of considerable length to allow the expansion to take place. Is this correct?'

'Quite correct,' said the shop-man, his eyes widening.

'The pressure of the gas must be enough to overcome the friction caused by the rubbing of the dart against the sides of the pipe, and prevent a degree of slowing down?'

'Excellent!'

'No doubt the pipe would have to be adjusted to the lung capacity of the user?'

'Oh, absolutely. Positively made to measure.'

'Ah. I shall construct my own blowpipe according to my own lung capacity.'

'Will you, though,' said the shop-man curiously. 'Don't forget that it might be difficult to use it in a confined space. Awkward in a bijou residence. You might sweep things off the mantelpiece as you took aim.'

'A good point. And conspicuous to carry about. I shall make it in sections.'

'And cart it around like a set of cricket stumps,' mused the shop-man. 'Well, good luck. I must say it's refreshing to meet someone who takes such an intelligent interest. I can't interest you in a boomerang, I suppose?'

'No.'

As Sir John left the shop, the shop-man raised his eyebrows and, on an impulse, slipped out into the street to stare after him. A man was peering through the window, wearing (for the day was mild) a white Sportsman shirt with a red and white spotted silk cravat inside the collar, and charcoal-grey stretch flannel pleat-front trousers.

'Can I show you anything?' asked the shop-man.

'Police,' PC Mogpuss, showing his identity card. 'Did that man who just left buy a weapon of any kind, sir?'

'Not exactly.'

'How do you mean, sir, not exactly?'

'He's going to make himself one.'

'Ah! Is he! Would you mind telling me – '

'Come inside, Officer,' said the shop-man.

'Mavis,' said Harriet, 'do you notice any change in Norman lately?'

'No,' said Mavis guardedly, fearing what was coming. There was a change in Norman, in fact; it was in his behaviour, and consisted in his kissing her at frequent intervals. They were chaste kisses, as light as a butterfly on a flower, although, contrary to the usual practice of butterflies, they always landed on the same one. 'Why do you ask?' said Mavis.

'He looks worried.'

'He always does,' said Mavis, now on the edge of a precipice.

'Yes, but it's a different kind of worried look. Something to do with Smith and Hoskyn. You were absolutely right about those two; they're partners up to the neck in crime. Norman knows it perfectly well, but I'm wondering whose side he's on.'

'Oh yes,' exclaimed Mavis, with great relief, 'now that you mention it, he *has* changed about that. You know, he used to say "Oh, them" as if it didn't matter. Now he's behaving as if it mattered a lot. Like, as if my nice cosy murder was going to be a real one, with people getting killed. It isn't fun any more. I like being his girl assistant, but I don't want people to get killed. But you're quite right about what side he is on, Harriet. He seems almost to worry more about Smith and Hoskyn than the people he says they're planning to kill.'

'That's just what I mean,' said Harriet.

'Mind you,' said Mavis rather dolefully, 'this girl-assistant lark is all very well, but like you said, murder's serious, isn't it? I reckon you're right, this rotten hotel is all make-believe, and people ought to take things seriously, didn't they?'

'Oh yes,' said Harriet.

She and Norman were taking each other extremely seriously, but, to tell the truth, she was beginning to wonder whether she wasn't being loyal to her own seriousness rather than to her true feelings. When one has sworn eternal vows, it is embarrassing to renounce them in a matter of days.

She felt that Norman had ever so slightly changed. The first symptoms of normality were showing. He had wanted to be normal, and she had wanted it for him, but now, with a twinge of dismay, she suspected that it had been his very abnormality that she had fallen in love with.

She sought Norman out, disengaged herself from

what she thought was a rather routine embrace, and tackled him on the subject of the murderous intentions of Smith and Hoskyn. He was attentive at once. (Was he, she fretted, glad to be diverted from love-making? Although her own ardour might be cooling, she didn't quite want his to do so, or at least – ref. St Augustine – not yet.)

With his knowledge of the future, even though it was losing its accuracy, he had a fairly clear idea of what the plotters were plotting.

'We've got to stop them,' he said sombrely.

'Yes, Norman, that's pretty obvious.'

'Ah, but how we should do it isn't. The obvious thing would be to go to the police. They'd catch them and charge them with attempted murder. We don't want that.'

Instead of protesting, Harriet looked at Norman with heightened sympathy.

'I think I see what you mean. It would be like setting the police on a children's game.'

'Yes!' said Norman, delighted to be understood.

'Still, it's a terribly dangerous game, isn't it? What about the victims?'

'They play games too.'

'Only word games, though.'

'No, conspirator games.'

'I see what you mean,' said Harriet, for the second time. 'Games, anyway. So what we've got to do is, sort of, blow a whistle and call "time"?'

'Yes!' said Norman approvingly.

Harriet felt the stirrings of new feeling for him. She could not define them, but they were favourable.

'There's a policeman in this hotel,' she remarked. 'Luckily he's the stupidest man in England.'

'He's important.'

'How?'

Norman shook his head. 'I've never been able to say,'

he said vexedly. 'The very thing I ought to know, too. Something has always got in the way.'

Harriet had a revelation. Her intuition, now very acute, told her what it was that 'had got in the way'. It was this. Fate didn't intend him to settle the matter. Fate intended someone else. Herself.

All unknown to herself, she had come to this hotel with a purpose. Mr Glossop had spotted this in her from the start, although he had related it only to himself. Sheer innocence and a crowd of emotions had blurred her sense of it. But she felt it strongly now.

PC Mogpuss. Thick, certainly. Excessively interested in clothes. Awestruck by the upper classes.

But a dear in some ways. He was an ardent defender of the rights of women. Of course, to believe that the rampant Hoskyn was 'downtrodden' was beyond absurdity, but it showed a nice nature.

He had once said, 'You will always have a friend in me.' She could appeal to him, if only she could find something to appeal about.

'What are you thinking about?' asked Norman.

'PC Mogpuss. You say he's important but you don't know how. You can bet he doesn't know how either. I shall have to show him.'

'How will you work that?'

'To quote yourself, Norman dear, I don't know.'

She would have to be a cunning, scheming girl. Mrs Hailstone said she had it in her.

13

'Excuse me,' said the Duchess, in the tiny voice of Miss Hoskyn, 'may I ask you a favour?'

'Certainly, madam. Of course, madam,' said PC Mogpuss, glowing.

'Good-ho,' said the Duchess, in the voice of the Duchess, clumping him. 'You don't ask what it is. Just say yes right away. You're a good lad. Well, I want to borrow a wheelbarrow. Er – for compost. For my window-boxes.'

The trained mind of PC Mogpuss perceived that this was a clumsy lie, and he looked keenly and sorrowfully at the Duchess, who he was sure was being forced into crime by the scoundrel who dominated her, but he was flattered to be asked for help.

'It's that gardener feller,' explained the Duchess. 'Cuts up rough when I ask him for things. Listens to you.'

So PC Mogpuss went with her to the gardener, who turned out to be more recalcitrant than ever, so much so that the PC had to thrust his identity card under his nose, forcing his face into the horizontal, while the Duchess prised his hands from the handles of the wheelbarrow. The truth was that the poor old man was infirm and used it as a walking frame. Seeing him tottering, the Duchess, who was not without some rugged fellow-feeling, picked up a nearby rake and stuck it under his armpit for a crutch. But she spoiled this kindly act by good-naturedly clumping him, leaving him sprawling on the grass.

She led the wondering PC Mogpuss to behind the niche house and set the wheelbarrow down. She had been about to ask him to lie down in it – she wanted to measure it for size – but he was wearing an immaculate grey chalk-stripe double-breasted suit with double vents and flap pockets, and it would be a shame to get that dirty. Very well, she would lie in it herself. But it was summer, and there were no fallen leaves to cover the body.

'Hold on a tick,' she said, and made her way to the gardener's shed, from which she returned with some sacking.

'Here,' she said, climbing into the wheelbarrow, 'chuck these over me.'

Deprived of speech, he did so. She crawled out beaming.

'Couldn't spot me under the sacks?' she asked happily. 'Might have been anythin', like a load of spuds, what?'

'Y – yes, madam.'

'Good-oh. Mind you, I curled up a bit. Might have been different if I'd been stretched out stiff, what?'

She staggered him with a matey clump and ambled off with the wheelbarrow in the direction of the wood. PC Mogpuss was horrified. Things were worse even than he had thought. What horrible influence was that brute exerting over this refined gentlewoman, that she should submit to lying in a wheelbarrow and being covered with sacks? And what were the implications of this degrading act? With a mighty mental effort PC Mogpuss nearly got it right. She was being coerced into killing Mrs Toothpeace, whose corpse she would trundle into the wood, covered with sacks, while the scoundrel Smith busied himself digging the grave!

Indignation boiled in the policeman's noble heart.

Clenching his hands, scowling, muttering to himself, he hurried back to the hotel. As he entered the foyer he encountered Harriet, who chanced to be dusting there. She took one look at his face and stepped in front of him. He had every appearance of facing Mr Smith outright. That would never do. Not knowing quite what to say, she stammered, 'Mr Peacey-Mogpuss, sir, I need your help.'

'Madam, it's not convenient for the moment . . .' But he never could resist a woman's plea. 'My help? Of course. But I am on an urgent case just now – '

'Yes, sir, and I know what it is.' Her grave grey eyes were full of significance. PC Mogpuss loved intrigue, and fell naturally into the appropriate dialogue.

'You mean?'

Harriet knew the stock answer to that one. 'That's just what I do mean,' she replied in a low voice.

She drew him aside. Mavis, at the reception desk, watched them with bright-eyed interest. 'I know you want a showdown, sir,' Harriet said urgently, 'but the time is not ripe for it.'

PC Mogpuss was thrilled. No one had ever spoken to him in this splendidly theatrical form before, least of all his sergeant, who had a way of playing things down.

'Why do you ask this?' he said.

Yes, why? Harriet was unprepared. 'Because . . . because things are . . . things are not what they seem . . .'

She thought this very weak, but it impressed PC Mogpuss and confirmed his suspicions. A woman's honour – Miss Hoskyn's – was at stake, and this young girl meant to protect it. (He had wondered why she had been present when Miss Hoskyn had borrowed the weedkiller.) But he protested: 'But I can't just stand by and let – '

'The plot is not yet fully hatched, sir. I am a room-maid here,' added Harriet with inspiration, 'and I have watched it grow . . . I have access to all sorts of evidence. I can collect it and pass it on to you.'

'You must not put yourself in danger, young lady.'

Harriet was touched. His heart was in the right place. She fluttered her eyelids at him. 'I shan't be afraid, knowing that you are close at hand, sir,' she replied, and he went away, full of job satisfaction, to slip into a silk dressing-gown with scarlet dragons on a dark-green background, and ponder on the matter.

Harriet walked shakily to the reception desk. 'Gosh,' she said.

'That was mega-cool, sweetie,' said Mavis.

'Could you hear me?'

'No, but I watched your lips.'

'It wasn't at all cool, it was downright feeble, but it was all I could think of.'

'It looked like you managed it, though. We've got to keep old Mogpuss off-stage, like, until it's time for him to come on, right?' said Mavis.

'Yes, right. Has Norman told you that?'

'Yes. This is a new twist to a thriller, isn't it, knowing what's going to happen and deliberately keeping it dark!'

'The thing is, we've got to give the thriller a different ending.'

'A non-murder is being arranged,' remarked Mavis. 'How shall we do that?'

'I haven't a clue. I'm waiting for inspiration.'

There was no buried animosity between the girls now. It was strange, but since Norman had set about making himself 'Normal' their attitude to him and to each other had changed. They were too good friends to be jealous. Mavis had forgotten about the imaginary Rupert Robert, and open-heartedly wished Harriet luck. Harriet regarded Mavis and Norman with newborn goodwill. If he flirted with Mavis, who could blame him? She was eminently kissable. On an impulse, she leaned down and kissed Mavis herself.

'You're off this evening, aren't you? Well, I can slip away for a bit. What say we investigate the niche house?'

'Real detection!' said Mavis. 'Oo yes, that would be lovely.'

Never before in the Ariel Hotel had so much pondering gone on. PC Mogpuss, in his dressing-gown, sat in the attitude of Sherlock Holmes and pondered a two-pipe problem, although without the pipe. Mavis, at the reception desk, pondered very prettily, and Harriet, laying the tables for dinner, pondered and looked angelic. Sir John Marvell pondered over a length of bamboo tubing, cut it into four three-foot sections, and muttered 'Ha!' at intervals. (The Duchess watched him with approval, but she was the odd one out here; pondering was not in her line.) Mrs Hailstone sat in her office and pondered fretfully, like one who has solved a complex puzzle all but one piece. And Mr Glossop, in *his* office, did likewise, tragically, for he was inclined to dramatize himself. He saw himself now as the doomed hero, withheld from happiness by a secret too dark to unfold.

But he too was changing. The change in him coincided with the changes in Norman and Harriet and Mavis. The Duchess had convinced him that his fear of women was needless, because she had been the very personification of his fear, and lo! when she showed up in daylight, as it were, there had been nothing to fear at all. And Harriet had brought into focus his vague conviction that a woman was to be his salvation.

He was more moved than he could say.

He stood up and contemplated himself in the mirror opposite his desk. It had gilt lettering along its upper edge: The Ariel Hotel, Mockery Hollow. Prop: R. Glossop. Suddenly – this happens rarely to people who look in mirrors – he saw himself as he really was. Short, fat, pop-eyed, balding. He had believed that his fascination was literally fatal, causing women to hunt him as an irresistible quarry. He saw that he had been very much mistaken indeed.

His eyes shifted to the lettering on the mirror. Yes, proprietor of this great five-star hotel. And he saw his own worth. One could be fat, pop-eyed etc. and still be a man of great achievement. But one had to know him to see past the image to the reality.

Mrs Hailstone knew him extremely well. She knew him most sympathetically. Since his accident she had tended him with loving care. She loved him, he realized, trembling. Hers was not the sort of love that is sung about in musicals, but a practical kind that understood his needs. She was much more than 'a beautifully balanced machine'. She was his ideal partner. She was *the* woman.

Mr Glossop flopped into his chair. It creaked under his weight. He could go on a diet and take exercise. When he had made himself presentable he would propose to her. Instead of running the hotel as his employee she would run it as his consort and his equal.

For a while he sat contented, contemplating a brave new life. But at last, like a reveller who awakes in a grey dawn, he was reminded of a deadly spite that would not go away. There was his name.

He knew now why he hated his name and he knew that this was silly. That made no difference. It was no good his telling himself to pull himself together. That advice never yet helped anyone with a phobia.

Mrs Hailstone would become Mrs Glossop. Two Glossops instead of one.

There was no way round this.

As it happened, Harriet had to work in the bar that evening, and could not slip away, but Mavis waited patiently for her, and they set out after eleven o'clock. They strolled down the brilliantly lit path of the Ariel until they passed the niche house, and then they doubled back and crept in behind St Phocas and the marble woman. They found the small area unexpectedly crowded.

Propped up against the back wall, gleaming in the light of Harriet's torch, were the hollow casts of the two statues. Smith had evidently made moulds of the latter with some kind of heavy-duty foil, and plastered over the outsides of them. The man was wonderfully skilled. These replicas were more perfect in execution than the weather-beaten statues themselves.

The girls were dismayed. Not surprised: Norman had foretold this. The shock was in finding the casts finished and ready so soon. Why, all that was needed now was to kill the Toothpeaces and encase them, and the job would be done.

'We really would have to tell the police then,' whispered Mavis. 'The real police, I mean, not old Peacey-Weacey.'

'Yes, we couldn't exactly forget about it.'

'We need delaying tactics.'

'But this is getting beyond a joke,' said Harriet, shaking her head.

'I don't like the idea of packing it in, though.'

'But if we keep this dark we may be called accessories after the fact or whatever it is. There's a limit to ev—' Harriet stopped abruptly. '*Sh-sh!*'

They heard the voices of Smith and Hoskyn, growing louder as they approached.

'Oh my *Gawd*,' breathed Mavis. 'Hope they don't stuff those cases with *us*!'

'*Sh-sh!*'

But the couple did not enter the niche house. The girls listened to their receding voices, peeped out, and saw that they had passed beyond the forecourt of the hotel. They crept out of the niche house and crouched down by the side farthest from the path.

'Let's scarper,' said Mavis.

'Hang on a bit. If they come back we'll play hide-and-seek with them.'

They crouched down, making themselves as small as possible, and soon Smith and Hoskyn came back trundling a wheelbarrow, which they set down in front of the niche house. (This pair, as we have seen already, had a fine aristocratic disdain of being surprised.) Smith squatted before St Phocas and, with substantial help from Hoskyn, tilted the statue over his shoulder and slowly, steadily stood upright. The eyes and mouths of the girls opened in silent amazement at this incredible feat of strength. Hoskyn now helped him to lay it gently in the wheelbarrow. They covered it with sacks and, taking a handle apiece, trudged off in perfect co-ordination towards the wood. A few minutes later they returned and went through the same procedure with the marble lady. Then they returned again and fished out something that the girls had failed to notice – a large placard, which they propped up in front of the niche house. Then they slumped down, leaning their backs against the plinths of the statues.

'Good show, Sir John,' said the Duchess.

'I couldn't have done it alone, Duchess,' he replied.

Now all this time Harriet and Mavis had known the pair only as Smith and Hoskyn. They stared at each other, suppressed a gasp, and remained with their mouths open like goldfish.

In many of the detective stories that Mavis had read, the villain would oblige by explaining in detail the whole course of his villainy, sometimes while holding the hero at gunpoint, and sometimes while, unknown to him, the hero listened from behind cover. This made for some stilted dialogue, but it was highly useful for the hero, who either kicked the gun out of the villain's hand or emerged holding one of his own, and could say with complete assurance, 'The game's up, Carruthers.'

To Mavis's extreme joy, Sir John and the Duchess now exactly followed this well-worn practice.

'Ha!' said Sir John, so pleased with himself that he repeated it, making it a triumphant laugh, 'Little does anyone know that you are the Duchess of Sligo and I Sir John Marvell!'

'Apart from the Toothpeaces, who will soon be unable to tell tales, bein' killed by poisoned darts shot from a blowpipe and turned into statues,' agreed the Duchess.

'Yes indeed. We've had our setbacks, having failed to kill them twice apiece – '

'With poisoned sherry, a huge stone pot, and two shots at implosion,' supplemented the Duchess, 'but this time we shall not fail!'

'Ha! no. I shall shoot them down as they pass the wood on their way to the village.'

'Good-oh. Is your secret poison, that kills instantly, leavin' no trace, a sure thing?'

'Absolutely. Today I shot a bird that was sitting on a fence.'

The Duchess broke into the expository conversation to say doubtfully, 'Shootin' a sitter! Not so good, pal.'

'The bird was a starling.'

'Oh, that's all right, then.' The Duchess now resumed the exposition. 'Got the poisoned darts all ready?'

'They are in a box in the left-hand drawer of my dressing-table.'

'Great. Well, we can do no more tonight. Let's go.'

The girls crept out of hiding.

'That was lovely,' said Mavis. 'Exactly as it ought to have been.'

'We still have a problem, though,' said Harriet. 'Somehow we've got to supply another ending.'

'Got any ideas, love?'

'Not yet.'

'Then we'll have to employ stalling-tactics. You tidy up

Smith's room. (Or I should say Sir John Marvell's.) You can pinch his box of darts and chuck them away.'

'I've got an A-Level in physics,' said Harriet thoughtfully.'

'Yeah? My auntie won some fish knives at bingo.'

'I mean I might be able to fix the darts and make them harmless.'

'Where's the point of that?'

'I have the impression,' said Harriet, 'that Sir John doesn't take to failure too kindly. I think if he fails to kill the Toothpeaces a third time running it'll shake his nerve and set him up for our alternative ending, whatever that is.'

'You're one of those psychological detectives,' said Mavis admiringly. 'There's one snag, though, sweetie. I should have thought of it before. You have to wait for Sir John to leave his room before you can tidy it, right? You can bet that when he goes he'll take his darts with him.'

It was not until Harriet was in bed drinking cocoa that she thought of an answer to this one.

'PC Mogpuss,' she said. 'He loves the Duchess and she loves him. Somehow I'll get him to entice her away for the morning. Sir John will never do the job on his own. It would have to be a team effort.'

'They make a good team,' remarked Mavis. 'They get on well, those two.'

'Yes, they do,' said Harriet, struck by this. The vaguest notion of 'an alternative ending' crossed her mind. But it was late and she was tired, and she fell asleep before she could dwell on it.

14

Norman now did his exercises at all times of the day, staring at his names until they became a blur that spelt Normal. He still found this boring, but it was the boredom of addiction, such as is felt by people who compulsively work slot machines. And it was having dramatic results. He could not place a horse any more, not even in the first three, and Ted Hughes was no longer in danger of being gazumped.

Norman was no longer in love.

The sentimental reader may feel that he was paying too high a price for his freedom. Lose his valuable gift? Fall out of an enchantment? What a chilly success!

But what a recompense. As the future faded from his mind – a sensation like loss of memory – so his sense of the present became more acute. He was still not strictly 'normal'. He saw the present too clearly. He saw through illusion and delusion. It was like waking into sunlight.

Harriet had said that the Ariel Hotel seemed to be floating on cloud, a dream palace. But this was true of the Ariel only in a special light, and only a few special people were in the dream. Most of the guests were not 'imaginary'. They came for limited periods and departed for no one cared where. But the principal players, those with names, they defied reality. They were like Alice's pack of cards. They were unreal in the head, acting out a charade. They needed gently waking.

But not by Norman himself. That task was Harriet's. He accepted this without rancour. Harriet had assets which he lacked. She had the kind of insight which is peculiar to women. Moreover (this was mystic but still a fact), fate had sent her here for a purpose.

As for falling out of love, he had fallen into friendship, a saner state altogether.

Harriet felt the same. She was no longer jealous or moody. When in love she had never really *liked* Norman. She did now, very much. She thought it strong-minded of him not to back certain winners, and noble of him not to write the poems of Ted Hughes before the poet could put pen to paper. She liked his new-found common sense. She enjoyed taking part in civilized conversation without being molested.

All the same, she rather looked forward to the time when she would be molested again.

Norman, in spite of his new enlightenment, looked forward to it too. Indeed, he was experiencing a new feeling. Hope.

'He says he wants to see me on an important matter,' said the Duchess.

'I've always said that we shouldn't meddle with the police,' complained Sir John.

'Oh, come on. Best way – make friends with 'em. Besides, he's a nice lad. Eats out of my hand. Anything wrong, old pal?' (for Sir John looked sullen and did not reply.)

'Not losin' heart, are you?' said the Duchess. 'Not after all the marvellous things you've done?'

'Luck has been against me all along,' muttered Sir John.

The Duchess did something unusual, for her. She put an arm solicitously round his shoulders.

'Come on, now. Never say die, what?'

'If I fail this time, it will be the last time.'

Never had she seen him so depressed. It weakened her own resolve, for to be honest she too was getting tired of this self-imposed project; but it would have been false to her nature to admit it.

'You won't fail,' she said gently. 'This scheme is perfect.'

Sir John roused himself. 'What important matter could he want to see you about?'

'We'll soon find out,' said the Duchess, and left the room, soon to return. 'He just wants me to help him choose a pullover,' she said cheerfully. 'See? Nothin' to worry about!'

'Why ask you? He's always buying clothes!'

'He was rather sweet. Said he valued the advice of a member of the upper classes. I thought he was one himself at first. He's not, but he's surprisin'ly decent. Seems that that room-maid put him up to askin' me – the good-lookin' one. She's too brainy for my likin', but a nice kid.'

'We'll have to postpone the plan, then.'

'Plenty of time. Keep smilin'.'

Harriet had persuaded PC Mogpuss that 'Miss Hoskyn' was on the brink of committing an act of folly that would ruin her, and had to be diverted. Her words were so thin and implausible that she was ashamed to utter them, as many a good actress must be when reciting her lines in a soap opera, but PC Mogpuss listened earnestly, and was charmed with the idea of getting Miss Hoskyn to help him buy clothes. He set off with the good-natured Duchess, and Sir John, after moping in his room for a while, went downstairs and brooded in the lounge.

Wearing her rubber gloves, Harriet opened the dressing-table drawer and found the box of darts. She was rather shaky, because she visualized metal ones that unscrewed, with the poison inside them. Unscrewing them with gloved hands would be awkward, and a slip might be fatal. But they turned out to be of very light wood, tipped with needle-sharp points that had been treated with some sticky substance for the poison to cling to; and next to the box was a little bottle that Sir John had conveniently labelled 'poison'. She now feared that the poison might be of some distinctive colour, but it was like water; and with extreme care she carried it to the washbasin and poured it away. It fizzed alarmingly, making her jump back, but she ran gallons of hot water through the basin and washed the little bottle thoroughly, scrupulously avoiding smudging the label. She filled it with water, screwed the lid on, and replaced it in the drawer. The Toothpeaces might be stung, but they were saved from being struck dead.

For the time being, that was. There might be another attempt on their lives. But Harriet felt optimistic. Things were working out. Nothing further could be done just now, anyway; and with Mavis at the reception desk keeping an eye on the comings and goings of the Duchess and Sir John, she went about, tidying up rooms, until she found time to call on Mrs Hailstone, being now completely in her confidence.

'Well,' said Mrs Hailstone – and, woman of the world though she was, she blushed a little – 'he says I'm *the* woman, Harriet. Quite an advance on being a mere vortex of efficiency. Of course, men always exaggerate wildly when they're in this state, but he thinks he means it. He's quite sweet, really. He's on a diet and he's doing exercises to make himself more attractive! He's lost five pounds! I used to think he was absurd – well, so he is – but I like him quite a lot really. And he's decided that he likes *me* a lot. And you know who I've got to thank, don't you? You.'

'I'm so glad, Mrs Hailstone.'

'Ah, but we still have a problem. It's like the snail

crawling up the side of a well – you know, he slips down one foot for every two feet he climbs. When will he get out of the well? Never, because that way he will never clear the top.'

'His name,' said Harriet regretfully.

'Yes. My being Mrs Glossop would only double the trouble.'

'Mrs Hailstone,' said Harriet, with great diffidence, 'couldn't you . . .?'

' – live with him without marrying him, like so many people today?' completed Mrs Hailstone. 'No, dear, I couldn't. For one thing, hoteliers have to be as free from scandal as any clergyman. More so, probably. Managers of pubs are the most respectable people in the world. For another thing, I'm a businesswoman and I like a contract. And in any case he'd still be Mr Glossop. I know it's ridiculous, but there you are, it's his hang-up and nothing can be done about it.'

'I wouldn't say nothing,' said Harriet.

'Wouldn't you?' said Mrs Hailstone, with a pathetic flicker of hope.

'I mean,' said Harriet, 'if only he could be persuaded just to *alter* his name a little – '

'Oh, I've thought of that,' said Mrs Hailstone, sighing. 'The trouble is, all the variations I can think of are just silly. Goggle. Gobble. Globule. He'd want something better than that. Did you know he covers sheets of paper with high-sounding names?'

'Go on?' said Harriet, guiltily.

'He'd like to be called something like them, you see. But of course they're no use to him. What would be the use of kidding?'

'I'm sure there's *some* name that would suit him,' said Harriet.

'Well if you find it you'll be my friend for life. I'll even send you a piece of wedding cake.'

Creators of the old-fashioned type of detective were right to make him belong to the leisured class, because it's an impediment to investigation to have to work for a living. Mavis was trapped in the reception desk and Harriet in the Ariel's rooms and corridors. Luckily they had Norman, on whom the responsibility for watching the actors in the drama now fell. Like all people whose place is naturally at the helm, Harriet felt uneasy about delegating authority, but Norman was a changed man and not in danger of falling into a trance as of old.

When the Toothpeaces left the hotel he went swiftly ahead of them, passed the spot where Sir John and the Duchess were already in position, and found a spot lower down in the wood from where he could watch them. PC Mogpuss also turned up, wearing a mustard collarless jacket, but he hid himself in the spot where he could neither hear nor see, and missed all the subsequent fun.

Sir John produced four sections of bamboo tubing from a cricket bag and fitted them beautifully into each other, while the Duchess dipped a dart in a bottle. He put it into the blowpipe and poised it for action. He stood immobile with the weapon levelled. St Phocas himself was not more still.

Hubert and Angela came down the path by the wood, with Hubert on the near side. Sir John adjusted the blowpipe. P-f-f-t! went the weapon.

Hubert yelped and clapped his hand to his neck, but did not drop dead instantly. He hopped about with more than usual animation.

'I've been stung! A wasp or something!'

Angela turned him round and examined him.

'You are in error. It was not a wasp – '

'Well, a bee or a hornet then,' snapped Hubert. 'Haven't we agreed to give up hair-splitting? In any case I said "or something" advisedly.'

'I mean that it was not an insect of any kind, nor are you stung, although excusably nettled,' replied Angela. She plucked the dart from Hubert's neck. 'You see? It's a form of missile.'

'So it is,' said Hubert, holding a handkerchief to his neck. 'Or one might say a projectile.'

'One might indeed,' replied Angela equably. But now Sir John had her in his sights, and a second dart struck her on the cheek.

She cried out in anger and, in extreme contrast to her old air of swooning, danced a brief and furious jig.

'This has been precipitated from some place of conceal-ment, or ambush,' she shouted. 'One need not ask by whom.'

'Sir John Marvell, or Smith?'

'Precisely.'

'There are flaws in your conjecture,' said Hubert. 'Sir John no doubt intended the missile or projectile for me. Why then should he strike (or wing) both of us? And as he presumably intended to kill me, why should he be content to achieve merely an annoyance, molestation, vexation, or nuisance?'

'Sheer incompetence.' Angela looked round about her, seething. 'Oh look, there he is!'

Sir John, aghast at his failure, had come forward almost into the open, with the blowpipe halfway to his lips.

Angela's voice came cold and cutting.

'If there were a Nobel prize for bungling you would win it,' she said. 'Not only can you not take no for an answer, you cannot even aim straight. Your second dart hit *me*! If you must use that silly toy, you should get in some practice with it.' She turned to her husband. 'Shall we resume our constitutional?'

'Or peregrination. Yes, by all means,' said Hubert, and Angela, with a final contemptuous sniff, took his arm and they walked away.

Sir John stumbled back into the wood, a broken man.

He did not mind being rejected by Angela, but the slur on his aim wounded him to the heart, for he had meant to hit both Toothpeaces, and he had succeeded admirably. Worse, the failure of his deadly poison dismayed him utterly. It must be fate. He sank down on the fallen log and held his head in his hands.

The Duchess came out of hiding.

'I must say,' she remarked, 'old anaemic Agatha showed a bit of spirit there. I didn't know she had it in her. Must be on a course of iron tonic or somethin'. Here, buck up, old sport. Never say die, what?'

'They never will say die,' said Sir John. 'Not by my hand.'

'What say we just rush them and clobber them?' said the Duchess.

'No.'

'You mean you're givin' up?'

'Yes.'

The Duchess sat quietly beside him. 'All right,' she said.

He looked up sorrowfully but with great relief.

'No one could say you didn't put up a show,' said the Duchess. 'You were terrific.'

'And you, Duchess, have been magnificent.'

'So what do we do now?'

'The least we can do,' said Sir John, 'is put the statues back in place. To leave them here would be discourteous.'

'What shall we do with the plaster casts?'

'Keep them I suppose. One each?'

'It'd be a pity to separate them,' said the Duchess. 'They make a good pair.' She paused for a long moment and added, 'And so do we, what?'

'We do indeed,' agreed Sir John, but being slow on the uptake, he did not see the implications of this.

'The statues ought to live together,' said the Duchess, 'and so should we.'

Sir John now saw the point.

'You mean?'

'That's just what I do mean.'

'Get married?'

'Good-oh, old pal. I see that you're with me. It's what Hubie would call a spiffin' wheeze.'

'Yes, a capital idea.'

'Gooders all round, then,' said the Duchess. 'What say we buy some sort of mansion and build one of those little houses in the grounds? Give our statues a home?'

'Excellent.'

'Marriage will suit me,' said the Duchess thoughtfully. 'I must always have had a hankerin' after it, or I'd never have wanted a twit like Hubie. And so must you, because that Angela is a joke.'

'I just felt the need to settle down,' said Sir John.

'Yes, it's time you stopped tryin' to prove yourself, old pal. Swimmin' the Channel, managin' banks and so on. Start enjoyin' yourself. Settle down with me.'

'With the greatest pleasure.'

'Good-oh.'

They shook hands. If you expected a kiss you simply haven't been following. Probably Norman, in a brief flirtation, kissed Mavis more often than these two were to kiss in all their lives; but everyone to his taste.

15

'He's gone all sort of practical,' said Mavis.

'Well, that's good,' said Harriet.

'Oh yes,' said Mavis; but listlessly. She found the practical Norman lacking in glamour, and the new situation flat. The 'lovely cosy murder' she had wanted was not going to take place, and the actors, according to Norman, were going to get married as if in any soppy love story. In fact everyone seemed to be pairing off and settling down to unrelieved domestic bliss. Anti-climax.

The girls faced each other across the canteen table and conversation flagged. Harriet, too, felt that the zest had gone out of life, but for a different reason. Something told her, even if it was not love, that the new Norman was necessary to her; but for all that their relationship was going to be under strain. She distrusted herself – she was soon going to university and a host of new young men. She saw the present pushing back the past, letters falling off, fire dying out. She distrusted Norman all the more. His job brought him in contact with self-pitying girls who fell for him as a matter of course. Men were notoriously inconstant.

'Cheer up, sweetie,' said Mavis, watching her. 'There's plenty more fish in the sea. Anyway, we're not finished yet. You've got to tell Peacey-Weacey all about it.'

Harriet stopped feeling sorry for herself. Tell PC

Mogpuss how things stood, all matter of fact? and he'd say, 'Oh well, that's all right, then,' and go back to the police station? It just wouldn't be fair, after all his time and trouble and many changes of clothes.

There might be a bit of excitement left.

'He wants a bang, not a whimper,' she said.

'I'm not sure that I understand that,' said Mavis.

'I mean he might believe me in his head but not in his heart. He wants a showdown.'

'You mean, like, something where he steps out and says "the game's up"?'

'Yes.'

'And then we rush in and cry "Stop! You're making a terrible mistake"?'

'Sort of, yes.'

'Oh, I'd like that, but how are we going to fix it?'

'Not fix it, Mavis, just let it take its natural course. Sir John and the Duchess are going to put the statues back. They won't do it in broad daylight – '

'No, in the dead of night,' said Mavis with approval.

'Yes.'

'What night will it be in the dead of?'

'I bet it'll be tonight. That Sir John doesn't hang about. What we've got to do is tip PC Mogpuss off, watch out for Sir John and the Duchess to leave the hotel, phone Mogpuss to let him know, and then scoot over to the niche house before they come back with the statues and hide until we can step out.'

'Then what do we tell him?'

'I haven't worked that out yet.'

'We've got to get our timing right,' said Mavis. 'Otherwise that Duchess will spill the beans. I never saw a more natural bean-spiller. And if she confesses to attempted murder, Peacey-Weacey will *have* to report it. It's a crime.'

'We'll time it all right,' said Harriet.

143

'And this is letting nature take its course, is it?'

Harriet smiled. 'Oh well, with a bit of encouragement from us,' she said.

PC Mogpuss was pondering again, having slipped into an autumn paisley dressing-gown (100 per cent cotton) to ponder in. He had been pondering ever since breakfast. He was worried.

He had one thing in common with Mavis: he loved old-fashioned detective stories, but more especially those that featured lords and ladies. Seeking that glamorous world, he had joined the police force. He was disappointed. Mockery Hollow was a docile place and his only contact with crime was to warn cyclists about rear lights, and his only contact with lords and ladies was being asked by tourists to be directed to stately homes. And then he had been put on this case at the Ariel Hotel and he had entered the world of his dreams. Here was a noble gentlewoman in thrall to a scheming villain. Using some diabolical hold over her, the villain was making her his accomplice to a dastardly murder. It was his perfect scenario. Perfection was added to perfection by his being given access to an unlimited wardrobe of beautiful clothes. He would have liked this state of affairs to last for ever.

What troubled him now was the relationship of Smith and Hoskyn. It had changed. At breakfast this morning they had sat together and gave no sign of being oppressor and oppressed. There was no mistake about it: they were friendly. If they hadn't looked so happy he might have taken them for man and wife.

And where had the murder got to? Angela Toothpeace was still alive and (as far as he had gathered from his muffled hiding-place in the wood) kicking.

And he still couldn't relate Smith to the odd things that had happened.

What about the blowpipe?

The shop-man in the village had told him some queer things about that, but you couldn't charge a man for merely showing an interest in an antique.

Had it all been much ado about nothing? Was he now to return to wearing that unbecoming uniform? No more beautiful clothes?

That would hurt most of all.

He ceased pondering and sat in a gloomy suspension of thought.

There was a tap at his door and Harriet came in.

'Excuse me, sir, may I . . . ?'

'Go ahead,' he said, quickening a little. This room-maid was the conspiratorial one.

His gaze followed her as she tidied his room. She was aware of it and was intent on keeping it there. She went into the bathroom and took her time cleaning it. She came out and dusted some more. Only after she had kept him in suspense for some ten minutes did she pause beside him and say in a vibrant whisper: '*Tonight*.'

He sat up, startled, unsure of what she had in mind. He was a virtuous young man. But Harriet hastily dispelled any doubts he might have. She breathed, more conspiratorially than ever: 'The niche house. The show-down. Tonight's the night.'

PC Mogpuss put on his keenest expression and rather needlessly produced a notebook.

'When?' he asked tersely.

This was first-class drama, and the real McCoy.

'I shall give you the word when they move,' said Harriet, equally tersely.

'You must leave trailing them to me. It is no job for a young lady.'

How chivalrous he was! Harriet cooed inwardly; but she said, 'No, sir. They know you're a policeman and if they spot you it'll spoil everything. I'm always pottering about the hotel and they won't take any notice of me.'

'But take care. That man is dangerous.'

'I will, sir,' said Harriet, and walked conspiratorially out.

PC Mogpuss put on a cropped single-breasted terra-cotta jacket and dark trousers and went buoyantly for a stroll.

'I think you teased him a bit,' said Mavis.

'Of course I did.'

'Didn't he ask you what the showdown was going to be about?'

'No, of course he didn't.'

'Do you know what it's going to be about?'

'No, I'm going to play it by ear. Get a fixed idea of what's going to happen, and it's all the more likely to go wrong.'

'That's not how Norman goes about things!'

'It is now.'

'My time's nearly up at the Ariel,' said Harriet in a muted tone.

'You've made your mark, though,' said Norman.

'Mr Glossop still has a problem. It's this snail-crawling-up-a-well thing.'

'Oh yes, you've only managed half a miracle there,' said Norman with a kind of envy. 'Do you realize that *I* was brought here to sort him out? – and look how far I've got!'

'Perhaps you will even yet, Norman.'

'I've got to get used to the word "perhaps"!'

'But that's what you wanted?'

'Do we ever get what we want?'

This struck a chord somewhere, and they were both silent for a while.

'Norman,' said Harriet, 'you will write, won't you?'

'Yes, of course.'

' "Yes, of course",' echoed Harriet with a sudden loss

146

of temper. 'But you'll have a few other girls on the side, though, won't you? Like you've had Mavis, for instance?'

'Harriet . . .' protested Norman.

'You'll forget me in five minutes.'

'Keep reminding me, then. Keep writing and I'll be bound to answer.'

'I don't think absence *does* make the heart grow fonder.'

'Then we'll have to do something about it.'

'Like what? Don't tell me – you're going to say, "I don't know".'

'That's right. But I'm not going to do nothing.'

Norman sat in the foyer and pretended to read a book.

There was no one at the reception desk at this late hour, but a press-button could summon whoever happened to be on duty. It was not Mavis's turn, but she had swopped with a gratified fellow-worker, and sat in her room waiting for Norman to buzz her. If some other guest buzzed her it could cause complications, but Norman thought this unlikely. It was curious that the other guests either kept in the background or weren't there at all when the drama was being enacted. They were like bit-part actors who played in crowd scenes or stayed off-stage altogether.

Sir John and the Duchess came into the foyer, looking pleased with themselves.

'Evenin',' said the Duchess.

'Good evening,' said Norman. 'Going for a stroll?'

'Oh, not far,' said the Duchess. 'We're goin' to – ' She would have told him, too, in her expansive way, but Sir John interrupted quickly.

' – look at the moon,' he said.

'You'll find it thataway,' said Norman, pointing to the ceiling.

'Ha! I like that!' said the Duchess, and would have

clumped him had he not been unclumpable in an armchair. She and Sir John went out arm-in-arm. They made a handsome couple, and looked so happy that to arrest them would be a crime. Please God, let nothing go wrong now. Norman crossed to the desk and pressed the button.

Harriet and Mavis were drinking cocoa and discussing, not the impending adventure, but Norman and their attitudes to him. Mavis had 'gone off' him. When moody, broody and mysterious he had fitted the cosy murder scenario to perfection, but as his new daylight self he was a square peg. Harriet felt as if she had missed the last train to some essential terminus. She had little faith in Norman's promise to 'do something' about their separation. That seemed just the feckless optimism so common to males. She was no longer scatty about him as she had been before, but as time ticked by she knew that she couldn't do without him. Both girls expressed their feelings very indirectly. It would be no good recording their conversation, because they repeated themselves over and over again.

Mavis's buzzer buzzed.

'Action,' said Norman.

Harriet rang PC Mogpuss.

'Action,' she said, with appropriate crispness.

Then the girls scuttled downstairs almost as fast as firemen down the station pole, beating the lift and trusting to PC Mogpuss to dress for the occasion to allow them to get ahead of him. Which he did, diving into Gant original blue jeans and a red blouson with leather sleeves, but in the urgency of the occasion he did this as speedily as a soldier affixing a gas mask.

Norman was on the hotel steps. Yes, all clear. Sir John and the Duchess could just be seen ambling off towards the wood. The three of them streaked across the lawns and crouched down by the gardener's shed, only a few yards away, and almost immediately PC Mogpuss loped after them. His manner of loping caused them some anxiety. They had expected him to dash straight to the niche house and hide – or better, perhaps, ensconce himself – in it; but he ran in a zigzag fashion, crouched double as if under fire, and the danger was that he might spot them as he weaved along. They meant to join up with him, of course, but not yet. He apparently did not see them, however, and was presently ensconced.

Norman and the girls made a quick dash to the side of the niche house farthest from the path.

'Sweetie,' whispered Mavis, 'can *I* say stop, you're making a terrible mistake?'

'Yes of course, darling.'

'What are you going to say?'

'I don't know yet.'

'Do you know, Norman?'

'No, thank God. Sh-sh!'

Sir John and the Duchess came into view, trundling the heavy-duty wheelbarrow, from which they lifted the marble lady and left her on the ground. They ambled away again. PC Mogpuss was caught off guard; he had been marvelling over the four halves of the substitute statues at the back of the niche house. But he was ready for them when they came back with St Phocas. He stepped out, putting up his hand as if halting traffic.

'A minute!'

'Oh, it's that nice policeman lad,' said the Duchess cordially. 'Give us a hand here, son, will you?'

PC Mogpuss was caught off guard again. He never could refuse the request of a lady. Pursing his lips, he squatted and took St Phocas by the neck. Good Heavens, what a weight! He could lift it only a few inches. But the Duchess assisted him, and Sir John squatted and took it on his back, straightened with a sudden jerk, and rocked it on to its plinth, the Duchess steadying it.

'Good-oh!' she said. 'Now the other one,' and the marble lady was dealt with in the same manner. The effort exhausted PC Mogpuss, who doubled up panting. The Duchess regarded him amiably. He recovered and, although the martial tone had been sapped from his voice, delivered his speech pretty well.

'Madam,' he declared, 'your ordeal is at an end.' He turned to Sir John, who was contemplating him with curiosity, as if he were an unusual insect. 'Sir, I am charging you – '

And now Mavis, prodded by Harriet, jumped out on him, but she was so excited that she fluffed her lines.

'You've got it all wrong, Peacey-Weacey – '

But Harriet dashed into the breech.

'Oh Mr Mogpuss, sir, don't be too hard on them, don't arrest them for a harmless prank – '

'*Prank?*'

Harriet still did not know what to say. 'Harmless,' she repeated, nodding frantically.

'You call attempted murder a harmless prank?'

'*Murder?*' echoed Harriet, and trilled with absurdly false laughter. 'Attempted *murder*? Oh, good gracious, sir, surely you don't think they're attempting *murder*?'

'Then what are they attempting?' demanded PC Mogpuss.

Harriet felt panicky, because the last-minute inspiration still had not come. But the Duchess reprieved her.

'Yes,' she said curiously, 'what are we attemptin'?'

Inspiration broke in. Harriet gave another peal of ridiculous laughter. 'What are you up to? Oh, come come! You're *collectors*!'

'Are we?' said the Duchess innocently.

'Well of course you are,' said Harriet, gabbling with haste. 'Everyone who comes to Mockery Hollow is a collector. Oh, you must understand, sir,' she appealed to PC Mogpuss, 'collecting is an addiction. It's a fever. This lady and gentleman took a fancy to these beautiful statues. They couldn't live without them. They craved them! They weren't stealing them, though. They just borrowed them to make copies of them! If you look in the back of this little house you'll see – '

'Yes, I've done that,' said PC Mogpuss dazedly.

'There you are, then. They wouldn't make copies if they meant to steal them, would they?'

'This kid's great,' said the Duchess. 'I told you she was brainy.'

'Most ingenious,' agreed Sir John, who had now grasped the point, 'I mean quite correct.'

'Then why did he make a blowpipe?' demanded PC Mogpuss, aggrieved.

'Why, that's another reproduction,' said Harriet. 'There's a fashion for reproductions just now. The hotel's full of them. Oh surely, sir, you can overlook such a little matter, can't you?'

Norman now intervened. 'Especially,' he said, 'when this lady and gentleman are going to get married.'

'*Married!*'

'Oh yes,' said Norman, taking over from Harriet, who was limp from her efforts, 'it will be a grand society wedding. This lady is a Duchess – '

'*Duchess!*'

'Of Sligo,' said the Duchess, nodding. 'And this is Sir John Marvell.'

'Sir John Marvell,' repeated PC Mogpuss faintly.

'The same,' said Sir John nodding.

'A member of the upper classes,' said PC Mogpuss, more faintly still.

'Yes, couldn't marry out of one's class, what?'

PC Mogpuss clung to the marble lady, speechless.

The Duchess clumped him, and he fell to his knees. 'You look a bit spavined, son,' she said, hauling him up.

'I don't know how to apologize – '

'Oh don't blame yourself, sweetheart,' said Mavis kindly. 'We all make mistakes.'

'I did tell you that things were not as they seemed,' said Harriet gently.

'Maybe police work doesn't suit him,' said Mavis. 'He's too sensitive, poor lamb.'

'Yes, a bit of a thoroughbred,' said the Duchess. 'Look, fix us some coffee, girl, and bring it to my room. For three. I owe you a good turn, lad. We'll have a chat.'

Mavis curtseyed. The Duchess and her husband-to-be nodded and smiled, and walked away with PC Mogpuss; but the Duchess turned back.

'How did you know we were goin' to get married?'

'Intuition, Your Grace,' said Norman.

'Ah! Like spottin' a winner,' said the Duchess. 'I've heard of people who can do that.'

16

'So that's our reward,' said Harriet, as they sat in the foyer. 'A gracious nod!'

'The posher they are the less they tip,' said Mavis.

'PC Mogpuss has done better,' said Harriet. 'He gets a cup of coffee.'

'But I expect he's had to drink that in the corridor,' said Mavis.

But she was wrong. As the girls and Norman rose to go to their rooms, PC Mogpuss came looking for them. He was flushed and elated.

'I'm glad I've found you,' he said, looking particularly at Harriet. 'You've done some running about for me, and I'm not the sort to overlook it. You shall hear my good news.'

'Promotion, sir?' inquired Harriet politely.

'Ha! Not the sort that you mean. I'm leaving the Force.'

'You'll be greatly missed.'

'Well, I think I can say that I handled this case pretty well. But as Her Grace says, I'm really too sensitive to be a policeman – '

'I said it, actually,' murmured Mavis.

'Her Grace says I'm a thoroughbred! How well the upper classes put things! I have done Her Grace some service – '

'Like borrowing weedkiller,' said Harriet.

'Well yes, but it's my *support* that Her Grace values.

People in her station appreciate such things even from the humblest of us. Her Grace remarked that I have good taste in clothes – '

'How observant of Her Grace,' said Harriet.

'Yes, wasn't it? – because really I don't think I've shown much evidence of it. Well! Her Grace and Sir John have wonderfully rewarded me – '

'Are they going to set you up in a gents' outfitters?' said Mavis.

'No, no! People of their breeding have no time for trade. But when Her Grace and Sir John are married, they will naturally run a large establishment. They have offered to make me – '

'An under-boots?' said Mavis.

'No,' said PC Mogpuss, frowning slightly. 'Their *Personal Haberdasher*!'

'Congratulations.'

'Can't call you Peacey-Weacey any more, can I?' said Mavis. She eyed him defiantly, but he did not take offence. On the contrary.

'That reminds me,' he beamed. 'You girls have both called me Peacey-Mogpuss on occasion. I shall adopt that title. A hyphenated name commands respect.'

'He's not so sweet now as he was before,' said Harriet when he had gone. But Norman said tentatively: 'Do you think Mr Glossop would settle for a hyphenated name?'

'Hailstone-Glossop, you mean?' said Harriet. 'I've thought of that, but there'd still be Glossop in it, and that wouldn't do. Oh isn't it tantalizing! He wants a name that gets rid of Glossop while sort of . . .'

'. . . keeping the sound of it,' said Norman.

'That's right.'

'*Words* have played a big part in this case,' said Norman thoughtfully.

'Yes?'

'What about Hailstone-*Glossary*?'

Mr Glossop was delighted. He rolled the new name round his tongue. *Hailstone* was sharp in meaning, yet melodious in its vowel sounds; *Glossary* was soft and sibilant in sound, yet pregnant in meaning, a partial dictionary. A perfect match.

He rushed to propose to Mrs Hailstone, so that he could assume the fine new name as soon as possible.

He was so liberated from his old phobia that he allowed sausages to be included in the breakfast menu, but he has never yet eaten any himself.

He and his wife-to-be invited Harriet to the wedding, but by then she would be in university in another part of the country. However, they made a note of her birthday.

Norman, having achieved what he had come for, slipped back almost unnoticed to (presumably) his old firm. He said goodbye to Harriet, but it was not an emotional farewell. He was curiously unmoved. He might even have been suppressing high spirits. Harriet busied herself with her final duties and refused to shed tears for him.

She and Mavis hugged each other and swore to be loving friends for ever.

They have kept to this so far.

Harriet went back to her parents' home in the village and waited impatiently for the last week in September and the start of a new life.

But a day or two before she left, Norman turned up.

Harriet accepted a lavish bouquet of flowers and kept cool.

'Good of you to come all this way when your work must be keeping you busy,' she said.

'Paranoics Anon.? I've left them. I've got a new job. Lecturer in a university.'

'What university?'

'The one you're going to.'

'Oh, Norman!'

'Don't look so amazed. My qualifications aren't bad.'

'I'm not amazed, I'm – I'm . . .' said Harriet, weeping. 'What are you going to lecture on?'

'Pericranial Percipience.'

'Whatever's that?'

'I'm not sure myself. Something to do with clair-voyance, I think.'

'But darling, you've lost the hang of that!'

'All the better. Those that can't do, teach. Although actually,' said Norman, 'I may not have lost it altogether. I still have premonitions of sorts.'

'What about?'

'Us, for instance.'